id

an honest critic.

THE PRICE OF REPUTATION

the second DI Kate Medlar investigation

Lin Bird

Tim Saunders Publications

Copyright © 2023 Lin Bird

All rights reserved

The characters and events portrayed in this book are fictitious. Any similarity to real persons, living or dead, is coincidental and not intended by the author.

No part of this book may be reproduced, or stored in a retrieval system, or transmitted in any form or by any means, electronic, mechanical, photocopying, recording, or otherwise, without express written permission of the publisher.

Cover design: Tim Saunders Publications
Image: Jingyi Wang, stocksnap.io

ABOUT LIN BIRD

"During lockdown I was able to devote time to a guilty pleasure — writing. My writing had previously been undertaken secretly and in snatched moments. As a former English teacher I have always been an avid reader and a lover of words for their sound and their meaning, both of which impact on my writing," says Lin. "I joined the Bedwas Writers' Circle and, with their encouragement, I began to seriously focus on my writing and on sharing it with others."

Lin is donating the royalties from this book to South Wales Blood & Marrow Transplant.

OTHER STORIES BY THIS AUTHOR

DI Kate Medlar Series

A Lesson in Murder

Other Titles

The Lift Book Club

PROLOGUE

The body was carefully wrapped in the cloth especially brought for the purpose. It looked like a chrysalis. No. Not a chrysalis. Nothing beautiful was going to come out of this cocoon. Perhaps a spider's web. Yes. A web entrapping the spider.

Carefully the body was lowered into the pre-dug hole and covered. With the trees so close no-one would be digging here anytime soon. Even if the growing new housing estate, marching across the fields, was to reach this border, the trees were under protection of a preservation order.

With a final pat of the earth and lofting the spade over a shoulder the figure, keeping to the hedge line, made its way back to the car, parked under more trees, these lining the cart track, the only access to this section of the field.

CHAPTER 1

DI Kate Medlar's phone rang as she finished her last mile of the five mile climb she had programmed into the machine. This early in the morning it had to be work. Kate grabbed her towel and wiped her sweating face. Her small stature and elfin haircut gave her a fragile look but her pounding of the kick box bag earlier would have shown that perspective to be wrong. Kate was not a naturally athletic woman but she had her eyes on one of the trainers at the gym. They'd met in an adult only swimming session, Kate's preferred means of exercise, and now, when Kate knew the trainer was taking an early session, she pulled herself out of bed for a glimpse and, hopefully, a chat.

The trainer was on the other side of the gym, helping a large woman master the cross trainer and Kate looked across, waved and pointed to her phone, mouthing, "Work!" The trainer acknowledged the wave and returned to focus on the woman on the machine.

"Morning Colm. What have we got?" DC Colm Hunter was her right hand man. He had smoothed her way into the Eashire community and they worked well together. A tall, well-built man who, at first glance, might be mistaken for plain and of average intelligence but all that would change with a smile. Kate knew he had a sharp mind and a winning way with suspects. He was an asset in so many ways.

"Morning, boss. Bed or gym?"

Kate shook her head. How did he know about the gym?

"Gym."

Her reply was brisk and Colm took the hint and moved onto the reason for his call. "A local farmer has found a body out near Knights' Halt, on his land. It's been buried."

"Right. Knights' Halt. That's east, on the Brightham Road. Yes?"

"I'll text you the postcode for your sat nav. It's a bit off the beaten track. And the final section is a beaten track."

Kate could hear the smile in Colm's voice. "I'll be there in forty. I must shower first. Have Mike and his team been alerted?"

"Yes. Forensics are on their way and the Prof has also been called."

"Okay. See you in forty. Good."

Mike Edwards was the best when it came to forensics and Professor Gus Lipstein was an amazing pathologist. The team was assembled. Once she knew what they had she'd talk to Detective Chief Inspector Bartholomew, Bart behind his back, and see what team she could put together.

Forty minutes later Kate was shuddering her way up a single, rutted track. This was where the sat nav had directed her but she was beginning to worry that it had sent her off course but then, round a bend, she saw a collection of police vehicles pulled up along the verge. She climbed out and changed into her wellingtons. It maybe mid-June but it didn't mean that it hadn't rained recently. A few cases with Colm had shown her that unlike the city, where she had come from, Eashire and its environs often needed wellington boots!

Kate saw the entrance to a field and marched through it. Across from her she could see a new housing estate, with the nearer houses still under construction. To her left was a hedge line and in the furthest corner a group of twisted and gnarled trees. Maybe six or seven, Kate guessed. Clustered at their roots moved white clad bodies and officers in uniform. The trees themselves were in the shade but shafts of sunlight illuminated the white covered bodies making them glow. Police tape cordoned off a large corner of this scene.

As she approached the busy hive she could make out the broad form of Colm in conversation with a smaller, wiry man. The details of his build were hidden by the white coverall but Kate knew it was Gus Lipstein. Both men turned as Kate hailed them and ducked under the police tape. "What have we got?"

Colm allowed Gus to take the lead. "Female, mainly skeletal remains. Judging from the presence of arthritis in her knees and right shoulder I would estimate her age as sixty plus. At present I can see no cause of death."

"But it must be suspicious for her to be buried out here," Colm supplied.

Both Kate and Gus nodded.

"How long do you think she's been here?"

"Difficult to be precise but I would say that the fact we've only skeletal remains, probably in excess of five years. Hopefully I can tell you more once I've had a closer look. I've left her in situ for you to take a peek but then I'll get her removed to my theatre."

"Okay. Thanks, Gus."

Gus moved down the slight slope towards the gate and Kate and Colm turned back to the activity under the trees.

"Colm, see if Alice Giles is available to do some research. Ask her to look at mispers for five to ten years, sixty plus female. See what comes up."

Colm turned away to make the phone call and Kate carried on to the grave but then turned back and called out, "Colm will you also go and talk to the chap who found her?"

Colm gave her the thumbs up and Kate turned back. Forensic personnel stepped aside so that she could take a look. Mike Edwards looked up from where he was crouching at the skull end of the space.

"Farmer found her. He wanted to put a fence

up to protect these trees from the final phase of the housing estate." He pointed across to the building site. "I think, like the grave digger before him, he had to start about here to avoid hitting the tree roots."

Kate looked around the open pit and saw what Mike meant. Tree roots were visible all around. This was one patch that looked comparatively free of their interference.

"Anything useful in the grave with her?"

"No. This is going to be a dental job if we are going to identify her. Most of her clothing seems to have disintegrated. We've got a few bits of synthetic, a zip and some jewellery. Not a lot to go on."

"Thanks, Mike. I'll let you get on. I'm going back to talk to Bart. I think we have to assume this is murder because she's here."

CHAPTER 2

"So, we run with a possible murder?" Kate clarified with Detective Chief Inspector Bartholomew.

"Yes. Use PC Giles to start and once you have Gus' report and you have more information we'll reconvene and set up an incident room."

"Thank you, sir. I did take the liberty of asking PC Giles to look through mispers for me."

Bart waved his hand. "No problem. Let me know what Gus has to say."

Back in the main open plan office Kate sought out Alice Giles. A young, enthusiastic and very efficient police constable. She was hunched over the computer and clicking through databases. Kate's approach alerted her and she looked up and smiled. "Morning boss. Not having a lot of luck with mispers."

"Have you looked beyond Eashire?"

"Not yet. I was just checking the county first. To be honest it's not taking that long as our missing person is a small statistic. I'm amazed at how many kids go missing each year."

"Female and over sixty. Yes. Not your average missing person. Right. Let me know if anything pops."

Kate walked away, weaving through desks to where Colm was sat at his work station, which was up against her own.

"Did you talk to the chap who found our body?"

Colm swivelled in his chair to face her as she walked up. "I did."

He reached for his notebook on the table and flicked through to the appropriate page. "Kevin Daniels, farmer. He's sold the property company, Eashire Homes, that field. Although it is in the contract with them that the crop of trees are under a preservation order he was not sure that the contractors were following all the rules."

Kate raised a querying eyebrow. Colm explained without reference to his notes, "Apparently there was some problem about a right of way. The contract said it would be honoured and the contractors built a garage across it!"

Kate nodded in understanding and Colm went back to his notes, "So he decided he would fence in the trees to make sure they were safe. He took his stuff up there this morning and made a start."

"What made him decide to dig where he did?"

"Apparently he was trying to stay close to the trees but avoid the roots and it was an obvious spot. He swung the pick a couple of times and then his dog started to go mad so he took a closer look at the hole he'd made and thought he saw something 'white and delicate looking'," Colm quoted. "Once he'd realised what he'd found he pulled the dog away and called us."

"So, do you think someone knew about the trees and the protection order and that's why they buried her there?"

"Well, as you found, it's pretty much out of the way. It would have to be someone who knows the area."

Kate agreed. "And they must be quite strong to get the body here, unless she was lured there and killed there."

"Well if Gus is right and we're looking at more than five years we're not going to find a crime scene are we?"

Kate shrugged, "Probably not but let's hope we can at least give her a name and let her family know where she is."

"Alice got anything yet?"

"No, she's going to widen the search. Someone must be missing her."

CHAPTER 3

Whilst waiting for Gus' findings Colm and Kate continued with their more mundane cases. A spate of burglaries in the Westergate area. The richest part of Eashire with its Victorian villas and modernist luxury homes looking out to sea or across the moors. Colm had an idea who it was, a petty thief called Kane Johnson, but proving it was a different matter. Johnson appeared to be forensically aware.

"Bloody cop shows," was Mike's verdict. And so they had little evidence to go on and were trying to track down Johnson's fence and work back.

Their discussion was interrupted by an email alert on both computers at the same time. Both turned to their machines. Gus had come up with some preliminary findings. Not least a name for the victim; Josephine Grace.

Kate called across, "Alice we have a name, Josephine Grace, will you call up information on her, especially family and who reported her missing?"

"Yes, boss."

With that Kate read the main findings. "As already stated, the skeleton is that of a female of sixty plus. The woman suffered with arthritis in both knees and right shoulder and has a healed fracture of her left leg." Then Kate's shoulders stiffened, "Fortunately, no small bones had been lost to depredation and so a potential cause of death can be ascertained: manual strangulation. The hyoid bone is still in situ and had been fractured across the horns. No other signs at this stage as to other possible causes. Subject identified as Josephine Grace through dental records. Oak Tree Dental Surgery, a local firm have been most helpful."

Kate looked up and noticed Colm scowling, "What's the matter?"

"Josephine Grace. I know that name. I can't think why but I am sure I do."

"Could you have been involved when she was reported as missing?"

Colm pulled one of his large hands across his face. "Maybe." But he didn't sound convinced. "I'll look and see if she had any online profiles."

"Won't they have been discontinued after all this time?"

Colm grunted, "Could be."

"Not necessarily," came Alice's voice as she walked across the office. She read from a printout in her hand, "Josephine Grace was reported missing in 2015, August 16, by her PA Claire Bayntry."

Kate looked puzzled, "But that's barely three years ago. Gus said the remains had been there for more than five years!"

"Well, I hate to disagree with Gus but

according to this report she went missing after a show party in August 2015 – three years ago."

Kate turned to Colm. "Will you get Gus on the phone and tell him we seem to be out on the dates and if he's got any explanation for the discrepancy."

Colm turned to his desk phone and Kate looked back at Alice, "Okay, what else have we got? Who was Josephine Grace?"

Alice placed a pile of pages on Kate's desk. "That's a very basic timeline of her career but in a nutshell she was an actress, or do we call them actors now? Anyway, she was a small time star of local stage and television and for the last eight or nine years of her life she starred in the local radio soap, Peaceford."

"An actress! What is or was Peaceford?"

Alice thought for a moment and then smiled, "Imagine Radio 4's The Archers meets BBC1's Eastenders."

Kate's mind faltered at the thought. Never a one for soap operas, radio or television, she could never get her head round how addicted people would become over their favourite. To Kate they always seemed to be storylines to slit your wrists to.

"Thanks, Alice. I'll wade my way through this. Would you see if you can track down next of kin, solicitor and something more about her life and character?"

"Yes boss."

As Alice walked away, Colm put his phone back and said, "Gus is going to look at the soil. He took samples anyway but is as mystified as us about the dates."

"That's one for the record books; Gus being wrong," smiled Kate.

"He's not taking it lying down," grinned Colm. "He said he would have an answer for us before the end of play today."

"Right. I am going to talk with Bart. We have a murder so I need a room and a team. Once I get back we'll set up the incident room and have a closer look at Josephine Grace."

Colm raised one hand in acknowledgement while the other was already clicking the computer mouse, hunting for information.

June 2013

Hello Sally,

I bet that's a blast from the past! How long is it since anyone called you Sally? Forty years or more? I thought it was time I introduced myself to you because I know ALL about you. I have studied and researched and left no stone unturned.

I wonder what your acting friends would make of Sally Price. Have you told anyone about your skeletons in the cupboard or do you just gather other people's? How will they react, these bosom buddies?

Will they understand the drive that made you lie and cheat your way to where you are now?

Shall I tell all? I may well do but first I want you to spend some time wondering when, where or how I'm going to do it. I want you to taste your own medicine. I know all about you Sally Price and it's not a pretty story.

I won't say goodbye, but au revoir because you will hear from me again, I promise. And, unlike you, I keep my promises.

I could sign off as a well-wisher if I thought my little missive would make you change your ways but I seriously doubt that. Let me be

Your Conscience

CHAPTER 4

Bart had given her the same room and the same team as for her last murder investigation. On the placement of PC Len Goodfellow Bart had remarked, "You seem to be able to get more work out of him than anybody else."

Kate grimaced in acknowledgement. Len Goodfellow. Definitely misnamed and certainly one of the laziest officers in the station. However, in fairness, he had made a very positive impact on her last murder case.

Room 11 was at the top of the station and although Colm had moaned about it being the hottest room in the station, Kate had not minded as her last use of the room had been in February. Now, in mid-summer, it was a different story. Windows were thrown open and Len detailed off to find electric fans.

The murder book was, once again, in the hands of Sergeant Hughes, a dour man who happily did his job and had no real expectation of further advancement. However, rather than making him bitter and/or lazy he made sure everything was done perfectly. No short cuts taken, no rules bent.

With Gus' preliminary findings on the wall and the discovery of the body by Kevin Daniels also written up, Kate asked for the information ascertained by Colm and Alice about their victim.

Colm began, "Josephine Grace, born Sally Price, January 24, 1952 in Finchley, London. Unremarkable academically but showed early promise as a song and dance artist and trod the boards at local clubs and pubs until she was fifteen. She left home in 1967 and seems to disappear off the radar until 1971 when she had a small role in a television drama. That seemed to be the start of her acting career and she went on to be star of the small screen and theatre. She never made it onto film and always claimed she didn't want to. She was also very unforthcoming about those missing four years, '67 to '71, claiming she was just being a jobbing actress and shop worker. But no details ever revealed."

Colm paused and Kate asked, "Are her parents still alive? Any siblings? Husband? Children?"

Alice took over the telling. "Both parents died pre- 2000. They had Sally late in life, but even when alive she had little to do with them. She had no siblings. She married and divorced twice and, at the moment, I can't find any next of kin. She moved to Eashire in 2009 when she took up the part of Lady Celia Frazer on the twice weekly radio soap, Peaceford."

Colm gave an exclamation and hit his forehead with his hand. "I knew I'd heard that name before. My nan listened to Peaceford religiously. There was a bit of a to-do at the time amongst the Peaceford aficionados. The writers had Lady Celia involved in a car crash and in a coma because no-one knew whether Grace was coming back again."

Kate turned back to Alice, "Do we have contact details for the PA? What about a solicitor?"

Alice held up a single sheet, "The PA, Claire Bayntry, still lives at Josephine Grace's cottage out Westergate way."

"Interesting. I wonder why that is?" Kate mused thoughtfully and then said, "Do we have a list of friends? Local or out of town?"

"According to my internet research, apart from her role in the radio soap, she spent her time very quietly, although longstanding friends from the world of showbiz did visit."

"Right. We're going to need a list of them. I think our first stop has to be the PA, but she can wait until tomorrow. Hopefully she'll know about the will and solicitor."

The others nodded and Len looked surreptitiously at his watch. Kate acknowledged that it was after five and there was little more they could do today, "Thank you everyone. We'll meet back tomorrow for eight and divvy up the work."

"Nothing from Gus?" Colm grinned.

As if on cue, the desk phone rang. Kate picked it up and listened. Colm watched patiently as

Kate nodded slightly, listening intently, before signing off, "Thanks Gus. Talk tomorrow."

Colm waited expectantly and turned to face Kate who answered the unspoken question. "Gus thinks the decomposition has been advanced by the presence of mycelium. Apparently, the soil samples Gus took show an increased number of them."

"And mycelium is?"

"Fungus!"

Astonishment swept across Colm's face, "Fungus?"

"Gus says he will be able to tell us more tomorrow but he's pretty sure he's right."

"Fungus." Colm shook his head and was still muttering, "fungus," as he left the office, throwing a wave Kate's way. She smiled as she watched him go. She was equally amazed but Gus promised to reveal all tomorrow.

CHAPTER 5

Leaving the station, Kate checked her watch. She had time to get to the adult swim at the leisure centre. Should she? She decided she should. A swim would be good for the tension in her shoulders and she might have a chance of talking with Jude. Perhaps even suggest they go for a drink afterwards!

The session was underway by the time Kate arrived at the poolside and it was very busy, as usual. She espied Jude in the serious swimmers lane. One lane of the pool was roped off for those who just wanted to power up and down getting their laps in or their calories burnt. Kate decided that she would spend the session just gently plying her strokes up and down and feeling her muscles release with the exercise.

A little after Kate began, Jude joined her, "Hi, I thought you weren't going to make it this evening."

"I thought I should, just to ease my shoulders."

Jude smiled and Kate was glad that the water disguised how much her legs wobbled. "I thought when you mouthed 'work' this morning that you'd be out of action for a while."

"It is going to be a busy case but we've got as far as we could today so I didn't want the team burning out on the first day."

Jude nodded and indicated the pool ahead. "I've done my power thing so do you want to chat and swim?"

Kate agreed and they began a leisurely breast stroke up the pool, avoiding straggling pairs and threes who were resting or talking on the side. Looking desperately for something to say, Kate asked, "Did that woman get her co-ordination together for the cross trainer this morning?"

"Yes. She did. I really admire her. As you could see she's a large woman but she is determined to get fit because she wants to donate a kidney to her sister's daughter."

"Wow! That's some incentive."

"Yes. I talked to the boss about giving my services for free if she comes in early on the days I'm in."

"That's good of you."

"No, not really. The boss says she'll give her free entry at any time – which is wonderful. I rang and told her this evening, she was over the moon. I got the impression that money was an issue."

"You ought to contact the local paper. A feel good story rather than all the doom and gloom they normally spray about."

"That's an idea. I might suggest that to Elaine. See what she says."

"Well it's got to be good for the centre's reputation."

Further talk was prevented by the sharp whistle blow. Their ten minute warning that the session was coming to an end. They were at the deep end and turned and made their way back to the shallow end and the steps. Already swimmers were clambering out and an orderly queue had formed at each set of steps. By mutual agreement they slowed their strokes even more so that the steps were almost clear by the time they reached them. For the final lap Kate tried to pick up the courage to ask Jude for a drink afterwards. What would she do if Jude declined? Would they lose the easy friendship that had developed? Simultaneously, they each cleared their throats and went to speak.

"Sorry, you first."

"No, it's okay. You first." Damn, Kate thought she was going to have to do it. Looking towards the steps rather than at Jude, she asked, "Do you fancy a drink afterwards? Perhaps in the café. You don't have to if you're busy, I…"

Jude's laughter cut across, "I'd love to. I was going to ask the same thing."

"Really?" Kate asked, turning to face Jude.

"Really." Jude placed a hand on Kate's arm and squeezed gently. "Shall I meet you in there?"

"Yes. Great!" At least she didn't need to wait around in the changing room. It was bad enough as it was, trying to avoid looking at Jude's naked body walking to and from the showers.

The café was typical of leisure centres

everywhere. A large window overlooked the pool, where now an aqua aerobics session was happening. Chairs were riveted to the floor and even the slimmest of people had to breathe in as they slid into the space between the seat and the table. Jude followed merely seconds after Kate and they mock argued about who was paying for the drinks. They eventually decided on Kate for the drinks and Jude for the carrot cake that Jude insisted was necessary after the pool exercise.

Sitting across from Jude, Kate now had a perfect view. Bright blue eyes, unusually framed by very black eye lashes. A sprinkling of freckles across the cheeks and nose stood out against a milky complexion. Her face was heart shaped with a pointy chin and the whole was framed by dark hair. Not quite black but not far off.

Kate was aware that Jude too, was assessing the woman opposite and they both smiled, a little embarrassed to have been noticed in their mutual gaze. Breaking the silence, Jude asked, "So how long have you been in Eashire? Coz that's not a local accent."

Kate smiled. "No, I moved here just before last Christmas."

"So very new to the area."

"Yes. I rely on my constable to get me to where I need to go. That, or the sat nav, but I don't always trust them as they have a tendency to take some very esoteric routes. Are you local?"

"Sort of. I was born and lived in a small

village to the east called Babbington Minor. I moved into town when I attended college. I worked in Chester for five years and then got this job."

"What was Chester like?"

"It was good. There was a lively scene and I loved the history of the place as well."

"You must find Eashire very different. I haven't found any scene. Is there one?"

Jude laughed. "No, not really. We'd have to go across to Bridgwater. Do you like discos?"

Now it was Kate's turn to laugh. "I do but I can't remember the last time I went to one."

"Well, we'll have to arrange a date," said Jude brazenly.

"Er, yes. I'd like that," Kate agreed. Feeling a little uncomfortable, Kate asked quickly, so is Jude short for Judith?"

"I wish! It's short for Judy, after…"

"Oh, not Judy Garland!" Kate giggled.

"Yep! Mind you Mum was also keen on Edith Piaf so I could have been Eddie!"

Kate laughed again. "Thank God my parents were quite boring and I got plain old Katherine."

"So is it always Kate? Not Katy or Kat?"

Kate shook her head vehemently, "Definitely not Katy. It sounds too…" she was lost for words, "I don't know – schoolgirlish."

"And not Kat. It would make you sound self-satisfied and your body language says you're not that either."

Kate gave a mock, "Phew!" and wiped her hand across her brow. "No, not Kat either."

They sipped their drinks and spent the remaining time in idle chitchat about their work, their colleagues and in Jude's case her flat mate. Soon it was time to go. They hugged tentatively on the steps of the centre and Kate watched as Jude strode away to the staff car park. There was a little flame of warmth in her being. Things were looking good.

CHAPTER 6

Kate met Bart on the stairs the following morning, "Ah, Kate. The media bloodhounds have the scent of our buried body and the Super wants to give out a media notice. What have you got? Have the next of kin been informed?"

"No, to the next of kin. We can't find anyone. This morning Colm and I are going to talk to the PA who reported Josephine Grace missing. Can you hold off on the notice until I've spoken with her and know who we need to talk to?"

"Yes. I can do that. Ring me once you have what you need."

"Thanks, sir. Will do."

As Kate walked into room 11 her team were assembled and Colm had gone via the local coffee bar. Four steaming cups were placed around the desk.

"Morning all. Just a brief update. Bart says the Super wants to give out a media notice but I have asked him to hold off until we've spoken to the PA. So, tasks for today. Alice you continue with the friends and family list. Len, I want you to look on social media and past media and see if Grace managed to upset people in her past. Colm, you and I will see the PA and then go and visit Gus about the fungi!"

Kate didn't enlighten the three who had

puzzled looks on their faces.

"Anything else from anyone?"

Shaking heads all round.

"Good. If possible I'd like to do a quick wash up at five. If that becomes impossible, I'll ring."

Grabbing her cup, Kate took the slip of paper from Alice with the address for Josephine Grace's last home, and left with Colm on her heels. She threw over her shoulder, "You drive. I could get us to Westergate but I don't remember seeing any cottages."

Kate realised as they drew up to Josephine Grace's home that it was not her recollection that was at fault. Calling Grace's home a cottage was like calling Buckingham Palace a town house. There was a semi-circular drive that could accommodate three cars nose to tail. Kate thought that this cottage looked like the kind of house children drew. Four square with four windows and a door. The only difference being there was a fifth window above the door.

Gravel crunched under foot as they stepped up to the front door. Kate noted, as she lifted the lion head knocker, that all the brass door furniture was gleaming. She heard her knock echo into the house and waited. She checked her watch. It was nine o'clock, if only just. As they waited she wondered if Claire Bayntry kept more leisurely hours now she had no-one to assist.

Just as she was about to rap a second time, the door opened revealing a middle aged woman, casually but stylishly dressed in grey, tailored trousers with a pale blue and white, loose fitting tunic. Her acorn brown hair was liberally shot through with grey and white wings were developing at her temples. Through heavy glasses brown eyes looked at them enquiringly.

"Hello. Can I help you?" Her voice was soft and educated.

"Claire Bayntry?"

"Yes?"

Both Kate and Colm presented their warrant cards, "Detective Inspector Medlar and Detective Constable Hunter. Could we come in, please?"

"Come in?" a slight pause and then, "of course, come in." She stepped back and opened the door wide.

They entered a light and airy hall. It obviously benefitted from the window above the door, which Claire Bayntry closed softly behind them, sidling past to lead the way to the back of the house, into a large but cottage like kitchen. A large scrubbed table occupied one end, surrounded by chairs. A dresser displayed antique, mismatched crockery and a butler sink with a wooden drainer stood under a large window looking out at the garden. French doors beyond the table led into a conservatory, which in turn led onto a large, well maintained and mature garden.

Claire hovered, clearly undecided about what to do or say next.

Kate took control, "Is it okay if we sit?"

Claire jumped into life, "Yes, of course. Please sit down." She drew out a chair and Kate and Colm pulled out theirs, opposite her. Claire's body language was tense. She sat forward and kept her clasped hands on the table. She looked intently at them both, her eyes flitting from face to face.

Kate began, "I understand you reported Josephine Grace missing in 2015?"

Claire gave a small gasp. "You've found her, haven't you? She's dead." It was a statement not a question. "I knew she wouldn't have just left. I told your lot that. She had to be dead. I kept hoping it was all a dream. I..." Tears were falling. Gentle, rolling drops.

Kate leant forward, "I'm sorry but we have found a body and have identified it as Josephine Grace. We need to contact her next of kin."

Claire shook her head. "There isn't anyone. Myself and her solicitor are her closest friends."

"Do you have contact details for him?"

"Yes, of course." She left the kitchen but returned almost immediately with a business card. "Gordon will be upset but, like me, he thought Josephine was dead, so it will just stop the unknowing."

Kate stood, "Do you mind if I step out into the garden to make a call?"

CHAPTER 7

"So there's no next of kin, just her PA and the solicitor."

"Okay, I'll let the Super know. Do you have details for the solicitor?"

"Yes it's a firm called Delver, Delver and Delver, now being promoted as 3D Legal Services. Apparently, Gordon Delver, or Delver senior, is who we need to speak with. Would you contact him? And see if we can have details about any will and bequests, please, sir."

"Will do."

Back in the kitchen, Colm had encouraged Claire to make a pot of tea, and a mug was waiting for Kate when she returned from the garden. Although mugs, these were beautiful bone china and each displayed what Kate would guess were hand painted pictures of native wild animals. She had a hedgehog, Colm a fox and Claire a fieldmouse. Briefly, Kate wondered if there was an unconscious message in their allocation.

After taking a sip of very pleasant tea Kate began, "Had you worked for Ms Grace long?"

Bayntry nodded, "Almost twenty-five years."

"So you must have got to know her very well?"

Bayntry nodded, more tears rolling down her

face, which she dabbed with a tissue.

"She employed me, temporarily, to help with her fan mail. She was really popular in the eighties and nineties. We got on well and so I became her personal assistant."

"Would you say you were friends?"

Bayntry hesitated, "I think we were close colleagues. Ms Grace was not a demonstrative person, and neither am I. I think that's why we got on so well."

"I know it's almost three years ago but could you tell us about the day Ms Grace went missing?"

Claire almost snorted. "Three years, thirty years. It's etched onto my soul. If only I could go back and change it all."

Colm's pencil hovered over his notebook. Claire shut her eyes and began. It had a rehearsed air, perhaps inevitable when something had been running around your mind for years. "Josephine had asked me to organise a show party. She used the excuse that it was the fifteen hundredth recording but in all honesty, Josey just liked a party." A smile touched her lips before she continued. "I'd arranged for the garden to be strung with lights and it was a beautiful summer's evening. Quite magical."

"Was it just the cast from Peaceford who attended?"

"Oh no! Josey was quite insistent that everyone involved with the show should attend.

The sponsors, down to the tea boy."

"We will need a list of guests. Can you do that?"

"Yes. All the details are on my computer."

"Did anyone else attend?"

"A few friends came down from London. She listed the names on her fingers: Gerald Purcell, Raymond Salisbury and Summer Loving. And of course Gordon Delver."

Kate had heard of all the friends. They were in the second tier of famous actors. Known but not stars. Surely Summer Loving was a stage name. No parent would burden their precious child with such a name, would they? "Was anyone else here? Did the lighting people stay on?"

"No. But we did have caterers. A local company, Gourmet at Home. There were half a dozen waiting staff and the chef."

"We'll need their details as well."

Claire nodded.

"So, what did Ms Grace do on the day of the party?"

Claire thought through and began, "She rose at her normal time, eight-thirty and had breakfast in the conservatory. She was ready for the chauffer at ten-thirty."

Colm interrupted the flow, "Was the chauffer Ms Grace's own?"

Claire shook her head, "No, it was a service laid on by the radio station. Josey didn't drive." As though that explained it all. Well it certainly gave Kate an idea of how much the station appreciated their talent.

Claire continued, "The car brought her back at about four-thirty. She went up and had a nap and at five-thirty I woke her with a light tea. Once she'd eaten she got ready for the party. Guests had been told seven-thirty for eight. Josey always liked to be ready for anyone arriving early."

"During the party were there any arguments or upsets?"

"No. It was a lovely evening. People wandered between the house and the gardens. Josey held court in the conservatory. There was laughter, chatter, music. Oh music! I forgot we also had a three-piece music group. They were in the garden under a small tent. It really was a magical evening."

"What time did the party end?"

"I don't really know. I had been on the go all day so at about midnight the caterers and music group had gone and I asked Josey if she needed anything else before I retired to bed." Claire shook her head sorrowfully, "If only I'd stayed up until everyone had gone."

"Were there many guests still here when you went to bed?"

"No, the bulk had gone. There were a couple of the cast from Peaceford. Gordon had already gone to his room. He and Summer were staying in the guest rooms. Ray and Gerry were organising a taxi but were still there when I went up."

"So, who were the Peaceford cast still there?" Colm held his notebook ready.

Bayntry closed her eyes. "There was Andy Watters and Christine Barford. They went on to marry and left the show to start an organic farm somewhere."

"And you didn't hear anything in the night?"

Again, Claire shook her head and broke eye contact. Kate's antennae tingled. There was something there. Had Claire heard something and now felt guilty about not investigating it at the time?

"When did you realise that Ms Grace was missing?"

"Not until the following morning. Knowing she had been up late the night before I didn't go to her room until ten. And only then because she had a fete to open at St Mary's, here in Westergate."

"Had her bed been slept in?" Colm asked.

Claire shook her head. "No."

"What was your first thought?"

"I knew she wasn't in the kitchen or the conservatory because I had been tidying up from the party. I'd checked the sitting room in case guests had wandered in with glasses and left them there. So, I knew she wasn't there. I assumed she was in her office. Well, sort of office come study come library. But when I checked,

35

she wasn't. I then went out to the garden and looked around. I didn't know what to think."

"What about Gordon and Summer? Were they up and about?"

"Summer had left earlier, about nine. It was her sister's wedding and she was keen to get to her Mum and Dad's, but Gordon hadn't come down."

"You didn't wonder if Ms Grace was in his room?"

Claire looked shocked. "Oh no! Gordon is a very old friend but they've never been romantically involved."

"So what did you do next?"

"I went up and knocked on Gordon's door. He opened it almost immediately. He was up and dressed and had been working on some papers. He helped me double- check the house and garden and then insisted that we contact the police."

"You didn't think that she may have just gone out for a walk?"

"No. Josey didn't do walking. And if she'd called for a taxi I would have heard it on the drive. She had the fete engagement and she would never let people down. I tried to explain all this to the police officer who came. He said he would alert officers to keep an eye out but you couldn't really consider her a missing person until she had been missing for longer." Claire looked accusingly at them both.

"Thank you for all this information." Kate passed across her card. "Would you be kind enough to email through all the information about guests and workers at the party please, as soon as possible."

"Yes of course. I'll do it straight away."

As the door closed behind them, Colm said, "She didn't ask how she had died."

"Or where we found her."

"Suspicious?"

As Kate climbed back into their car, she replied, "Not sure at this stage but I am sure we will be back to talk to Ms Bayntry."

CHAPTER 8

As Kate headed to the car she heard an alert from her phone informing her that an email had arrived. Waiting until they were both ensconced in the car, she opened it up and read.

"Mike has sent through a preliminary report. Basically they've recovered a dress zipper, a pair of earrings, two rings and a bra fastener. There is also evidence of some form of synthetic material, which may have once been red."

"Has he sent photos?"

"Yes. I'll send it across to you and then alert the team to stuff they need to follow through on."

Whilst Colm fiddled with his phone and then started scrolling through the email Kate had forwarded, she rang the office. Len Goodfellow answered.

"Ah Len, just the person I needed. You've got an eye for detail," a bit of an overstatement but he had found a crucial piece of evidence that others had missed on her last case. "Will you compare the description Claire Bayntry gave of what Josephine Grace was wearing when she disappeared and compare it with the report Mike has just emailed through."

"Yes, boss."

"If there are no details about jewellery,

call Claire Bayntry and see if she remembers anything. Is Alice there?"

"Yes, I'll pass you over."

There was distant rustling and a clunk before Alice's voice, "Yes, boss?"

"Claire Bayntry should be sending through an email for all those present at the last show party our victim held. Will you start by finding contact details and then cross referencing with media coverage?"

"Okay. Anything else?"

"Yes. Before you do that, track down two of the cast who left the show just after our victim's disappearance: Andy Watters and Christine Barford. I don't know if those are their real names or just professional ones. They got married. Supposed to be somewhere doing organic farming."

Kate could hear Alice talking under her breath, making a note of the details. "Okay, boss. I'll get right on it."

"Thanks. Colm and I are off to talk with Gus now. He's had time to examine the remains and then we'll head for REAl Radio (Radio Eashire Alive). Kate thought it a clumsy acronym but there it was. Text me through the producer's name and who the main players are in the show."

"Will do. See you later."

The phone went dead and Kate looked at Colm who had placed his phone back in his pocket. "Thoughts?"

"Well, I doubt the murder was for money. Those rings must be worth a fortune. Did you see the size of that emerald?"

"Yes. It doesn't make sense to bury them, unless our murderer thought they would be too difficult to dispose."

"No, I don't buy that. It would be easy enough to prise the gems out and sell them separately. They'd only be recognised as a whole, not as individual pieces."

"Umm," Kate agreed. "What about the material?"

Colm gave a short bark or exclamation, "I'm surprised Mike hazarded a guess at the colour. It's just strands. He says it was found on and under the torso, perhaps a cardigan?"

Kate shook her head. "No. Two things. Firstly, I think any wool products Grace owned would have been pure wool, not some synthetic blend. Two, I can't see someone like her wearing a cardigan. I think it's more likely to have been a shawl. Perhaps a silk."

Colm shrugged and smiled, "I bow down to your sartorial superiority!"

Kate play thumped his arm. Since her dress sense consisted of smart dark trousers with matching jackets and a clean shirt, her *sartorial experience* was decidedly wanting.

"Okay, head for the morgue and I'll give Gus a ring."

Colm switched the engine on and slipped

crunchily off the gravel drive whilst Kate called Gus. She got his secretary who confirmed that Gus could be available in about half an hour. "Perfect. Thank you. Please tell him we're on our way."

CHAPTER 9

Kate smiled at the receptionist as they entered the foyer of the morgue. She thought it must be a tough job because the majority of people who came through those doors were coming to see a dead loved one. Kate thought she wouldn't be able to cope with that much grief each and every day. However, the receptionist smiled in return and said, "Gus is expecting you in his usual theatre room."

"Thanks."

As they walked along the electric light-lined corridor the smell of disinfectant attacked their senses. It was so strong that Kate was sure she was tasting it. Arriving at Gus' room she knocked and poked her head through. Gus was there, where he always was, with a body on a trolley, waiting for Gus to detail the history the body told.

"Ah, DI Medlar and DC Hunter. How lovely to see you." He looked down at the sheeted body and said, "We have quite a conundrum here but I think I've solved it." The intelligent eyes behind the lenses twinkled and his eyes creased. Kate was sure he was smiling but his mouth was hidden by a mask.

Waving the papers in his hand, Gus began, "Just to confirm that these are the remains of

Josephine Grace, sixty-three years old at the time she was reported missing in August 2015. The hyoid bone was in place but fractured suggesting the cause of death as manual strangulation."

"Could it have been fractured whilst in the ground?" Colm asked.

"Unlikely. Apart from the disturbance at the top of the skull nothing had moved the corpse to cause that kind of fracture. Gus checked the paper in front of him. "Now, although there is some evidence of adipose tissue on some of the larger sections of the body, by and large, this is just skeletal remains. However, the rate of decomposition is not commensurate with the time she has been in the ground." He paused and looked up, "Thus my estimate of how long she had been there was out by a large margin."

Kate and Colm nodded in unison. When was he going to get to the why?

But Gus was not to be rushed. "At first I thought it must be the composition of the soil. Perhaps particularly acidic. However, samples I had taken from both the grave and the area around it, did not confirm this." He moved through the papers and selected one to bring to the fore. "However, what I did notice was the abundance of mycelium."

"Fungi?" Colm questioned.

"Well, technically, it is the root of the fungi. They form a web of strands under the surface of the soil. It is believed that some mycelium webs are miles wide and that they can communicate to one another."

Colm snorted and then apologised as Gus glared at him. "Sorry Gus, it just sounds a little…" He tried to find an acceptable word, "Strange."

"Fortunately for you," he pointed at the pair of them, "I recently read an interesting article about mycelium coffins. Some bright spark has grown webs of mycelia, dried them out in a coffin form and then buried bodies in them. The presence of the mycelia means that natural products are broken down more quickly, as the fungi use the body as a food source to grow."

Kate rubbed her nose, a sure sign that she was confused. "So are you saying that the mycelia just happen to be present and sped up decomp or that our murderer introduced them to do that work?"

"I would say the latter. The soil type and the general environment around the trees is not a natural place for fungi, which is why there was so little evidence on the surface."

"So would this take specialist knowledge? To produce enough mycelia for the job?"

Gus put his papers down and leant against the trolley on which the sheet rested. "Not especially. We can all grow mushrooms, can't we?"

Kate nodded, hesitantly. She thought she knew the basic application, "I suppose so." She paused to gather her thoughts. "Could the murderer just have thrown in some mushrooms with the body?"

"Unlikely. My guess would be that the murderer had either a mycelium coffin or material and used it to wrap or put the body in."

Colm broke in, "How many people would know about these properties? Isn't that quite specialised?"

Gus paused, thinking. "The general public are unaware. I was unaware, until I put my thinking cap on, but stuff like this crops up in universities all the time. Eco- warriors trying to find sustainable processes. So rare but not unknown."

Kate tried to gather her thoughts. "So this was pre-meditated murder? Our murderer had prepared this quite thoroughly before the actual event."

Gus nodded and Colm added, "And they must have local knowledge. To find the field in the first place and secondly to know that the trees were protected from the house builders. That estate had already started being built in 2015. Locals knew the whole field was up for development."

Kate nodded thoughtfully. "They could have thought that the body would have already disappeared by the time the developers were on the doorstep. But no. I think you're right. They knew those trees were protected. That's why the grave is as close to them as it is."

Gus placed his papers into a folder, a signal

that he had said his piece.

Kate took the hint, "Thank you, Gus. That was very interesting. We'll get out of your hair now."

CHAPTER 10

"Now there's a turn up for the books," said Colm as they climbed back into the car. "We've just got to find a university educated eco-warrior who knows how to grow mushrooms!"

Kate smiled, "Simple!" She pulled out her phone, "I'll just check in with Alice. Let's see what we've got so far."

Alice answered. Kate put it on speaker.

"Hi Alice, what have you got for us?"

"The Executive producer is called Anthony Rainsford but he's out of the country at the moment, until next Thursday. However, when I spoke with his secretary she suggested that if we wanted to talk to people who actually had day-to-day dealing with Ms Grace then we'd be better off talking to the show's producer, Sally Grey."

Kate was pleased to see that Colm had his notebook out, writing.

"Yes. I've spoken directly to her and she is available at lunchtime. She also suggested that she bring along the two main script writers."

"Main script writers?" Kate had always thought shows were written by one person.

"Yes. Apparently there is a team of them but these two develop the storylines and have final say as to what is included."

"Okay. Names?"

"Suzy Lambert and Anna Gifford. I've done a check on all three women but nothing has shown up so far. They all have mentions in media focused publications but nothing personal and nothing directly linked to Josephine Grace."

"Thanks, Alice. That's great. Did you mention the finding of the body?"

"No, I just said that we were taking another look at an unsolved case."

"Good." There were enough programmes on television now, fiction and fact, that a cold case being reopened would not strike the public as something abnormal.

"Speak later. Text if there's anything urgent."

"Will do boss."

Colm slipped his notebook away and started the engine, "REAl Radio?"

"Yes."

When they arrived at the radio station Kate thought she could be forgiven for thinking that they were at the wrong address. The station was based in one of those pre-fab steel frame and fabricated units so popular with out of town shopping centres or light industry estates. To the left of it were a tile shop and a bathroom fitters. Opposite was a carpet shop, a builder's merchant and a double glazing retailer.

The parking spaces in front of the building were full so Colm parked in the area for the tile shop, which was virtually empty. Automatic doors whispered open as they strode into the reception area. The receptionist, a woman in her late forties, looked up and asked, "Can I help you?"

Kate and Colm held up their badges and Kate asked for Sally Grey. The receptionist became super-efficient, or as far as Kate was concerned, super obstructive.

"You're not in the visitors' log. Is Ms Grey expecting you?"

Her attitude riled Kate and she spoke quietly but distinctly, bending forward across the desk a little, "As it happens, she is but even if she wasn't she will see us as we are here on police business, not some autograph hunt!"

The woman back tracked remarkably quickly, "Of course. Please take a seat." She pointed to a small alcove in which a range of brightly coloured chairs and stools were collected, "I'll let her know you're here."

Kate didn't hear the conversation she had with the person on the line but she called across a few seconds later. "She's on her way down."

Kate merely nodded. Only a minute or so later Kate heard the hum of a lift and the swish of a door opening, followed by a staccato click of high heels. Sally Grey was a thirty something with the look of the Sloane Rangers about her, right down to the pearls at her throat and the cardigan draped across her shoulders.

Grey looked between Kate and Colm, "Detective Inspector Medlar?"

Kate stepped forward and held out her hand to shake. "Yes. Thank you for seeing us at such short notice."

"No problem. I've taken the liberty of arranging some lunch with all three of us, Suzy and Anna, so that we can chat and eat. Is that all right or do you need to talk with us individually?"

Kate smiled, "That's very thoughtful of you. All together is fine. Should we need to talk more and separately we can arrange that."

Grey led them to the lift and wrapped her cardigan tighter around herself. She explained, "I know it's a lovely day out but the air conditioning in this place always makes me feel cold."

The lift stopped at the third floor and a long corridor stretched before them. With practised ease, Grey gave a guided tour pointing out rehearsal rooms, studios and the live studio as they passed. Finally, they stopped in front of a door with Grey's name on it. "Here we are."

CHAPTER 11

The office was not one of the largest Kate had seen but it did have an amazing view across newer Eashire to the oldest building, the medieval church of St Mary's. In front of the window a round table, set for six, was already occupied by two women.

"This is Suzy," Grey indicated a small, plump woman with dark hair blending into red tips, "and this is Anna." Anna Gifford was an older woman. Kate reckoned that she had a good decade on both the other two.

Introductions made, there was a knock at the door and a young man wheeled in a trolley. Small water urns on top, plates of food in the middle and plates, cups and saucers on the bottom. "Thank you, Ian," said Grey. "I'll ring down when we're finished." Saying nothing, the man left.

"Help yourselves to food and drink," said Grey spreading her hands wide.

For a few minutes there was just the mumbles of thank yous and excuse me's as everyone selected their food and drink. When they were all finally sat down and eating, Kate began. "What were your thoughts when Josephine Grey went missing?"

She looked from face to face. Grey had stopped chewing, Suzy carried on and swallowed and Anna took a sip of her drink.

Grey spoke first. "I think we were all mystified," she looked for confirmation to the other two, both of whom nodded their agreement. Grey continued. "It was so out of character. Say what you will about her, Josey was always a professional and she would never have just gone off without telling someone."

"So, what do you think happened to her?"

Anna came in, "I don't want to sound melodramatic but I suspected foul play."

"Really? Anyone in particular?"

Anna coughed on her sandwich and blushed a little, "Well, no. I just meant that I thought someone, a stranger, had murdered her."

"What and taken her body away?" This was Suzy who sounded scornful. "There was more to Josey than she ever let anyone see. I think she's gone off somewhere with someone."

Grey shook her head, "No! That doesn't make sense."

Kate allowed them to bat the ideas around amongst themselves but the long and short of it was that they had no idea what had happened to their colleague.

Feeling that the conversation was starting to go in circles, Kate directed the flow again.

"How did Josey get on with the cast members? How did she get on with you?" Kate turned and looked at Grey who stopped eating and looked thoughtful. "She was always very professional. She took direction well but would also argue her case if she thought I'd got it wrong."

"Would you say you were friends?"

Again Grey thought, "No, not friends. Professional colleagues."

"What about you as writers?" Kate turned to the other two.

Suzy looked down at her plate, so Anna took control of the conversation. "On the whole she was fine. Some of them would argue black is white if it got them a longer speech and more air time, but not Josey. Once in a while she'd ask about a particular word or phrase."

"Did you always give in to her? I mean did she have a point?" Colm asked.

"Sometimes. There was no hard and fast rule."

"How did Josey come to be in Peaceford, here in Eashire?" Kate enquired.

Grey smiled, "That was my doing. I'd heard on the grapevine that Josey was looking to move out of London but didn't want to retire completely from acting. So I approached her. I explained I wanted a lady of the manor type, with a practical, straight talking approach but with the assurance and manners of someone used to being top of the tree and always right."

Colm laughed, "Lady Celia Fraser to a tee."

Grey's smile broadened, "Are you a fan of our programme, Mr Hunter?"

Colm shook his head, "Not really, but my nan was an avid listener and so I sometimes heard it if I went visiting."

"Oh how wonderful!" Kate almost expected Grey to clap her hands in glee. "You must take some souvenirs back with you."

Grey had clearly not noticed the tense Colm had used, "Thank you, that's a kind thought, but she died a few years back."

Grey blushed, "Oh I'm sorry."

Colm waved a hand, "No problem."

Kate got the conversation back on track, "Did Ms Grace have any particular friends amongst the cast?"

They all looked thoughtful and then Anna offered, "Well she was quite pally with Hugh Gifford, he plays Celia's husband, George Fraser."

Suzy interrupted, "Yes, but that didn't last very long, did it? I noticed him, on more than one occasion, shooting daggers at her."

"I never noticed," said Anna thoughtfully.

"No, I think Suzy's right. They must have had a falling out before the second summer Josey was here because he didn't want to sit next to her at the cast bash at that Greek place."

"Anyone else?" Kate prompted.

"She was very close to a couple of the younger cast members. I think she was a sort of agony aunt. Both with their professional and personal lives," Grey said.

Anna added, "And it was thanks to Josey that

Summer Loving got her break in London."

"Did Summer Loving start off here in Eashire?" asked Kate.

"Not only here in Eashire but here in REAl Radio in Peaceford," added Suzy.

Well, there was a turn up for the books, thought Kate. A famous stage and screen star started life on a local radio soap.

"Who else did she mentor?" asked Colm, pencil ready.

"There was Tamara Cullen, she plays the vicar's wife now. She's been with us for five, or is it six years? She'd never done radio acting before and I know Josey was very helpful to her. Even had her over to her cottage to practice!" answered Anna.

"And of course Stephen was briefly her companion wasn't he?" Suzy asked Grey.

"Stephen?" Kate queried.

"Yes, Stephen Osborne. The vet in the show. Had a pedigree in acting before Peaceford but he and Josey were very close for a short time."

"Close as in romantically?" asked Kate.

"Oh no," Grey reassured her.

"Josey said she'd had enough of men when she divorced her second husband. Stephen was just an escort from time to time. Theatre engagements, that sort of thing," explained Suzy.

Any further discussion was prevented by the telephone on the desk ringing out.

"Excuse me. If it's my office phone, I have to

take it."

Kate nodded and they all looked nonchalantly around the room, not wanting to appear to be listening but in such a small space not being able not to.

"Yes. Okay. Tell him to relax. I'll come down straight away."

Grey replaced the phone and looked at Kate, "I'm really sorry but there's a glitch in the sound recording studio," she turned her gaze to Suzy and Anna, "Colin thinks Richie may have wiped this week's programme, again!"

Anna put her head in her hands, "What's wrong with that boy?"

"Are you going to ask Mark to have a play?" asked Suzy.

Grey nodded and returned her gaze to Kate, "I'll be back as soon as I can, promise." Kate nodded. She could have come heavy handed and insisted that Grey stay, but not now. Later, if she needed to.

CHAPTER 12

Suzy and Anna shifted in their seats and seemed to feel less confident with Kate and Colm, now that Grey had left.

To lighten the mood, Colm asked, "I got the impression that Richie has done this before? Who is he?"

"Richie Kershaw, he's an apprentice in the sound studio," began Anna.

"He can't still be an apprentice. He's been here for three, four years?" interrupted Suzy.

Anna shrugged, "Anyway he's a junior technician. And this is not the first time."

"In fairness, the last time he did it was years ago when he was really just an apprentice. And Mark did manage to retrieve it."

"Good for him, all the cast members who would need to redo their scenes would have strung him up. You know there's no love lost between technical and artistic!" Anna sounded heated.

"Did Josey get on with the technical staff?" Colm asked.

Both women sat thoughtfully and then Suzy offered, "Generally technical and artistic are separate but I think Josey was particularly kind to Richie. Young man, dropped out of university, new to the place, lowest of the low in the pecking order. I think she mothered him a bit. Don't you, Anna?"

"Yes." She sounded the word out to make it longer. Something was clearly on her mind and Kate prompted her.

"Is there something specific that you're thinking of?"

Anna looked at Kate and brought her focus back to the present. "I haven't thought about this before. Not even when Josey first went missing but I'm pretty sure they'd had a disagreement, Josey and Richie, the night she was last seen."

Kate waited for her to elaborate. "We'd just finished the special episode and everyone was keen to get off and have a rest and time to glam up for Josey's party, so within minutes the studio was empty. I was on my way to my writing room when I realised I'd left my script in the recording studio so I went back to get it." She glanced over Kate's left shoulder, "Richie and Josey were in the recording booth itself and Richie seemed to be having an argument with her."

Before Kate could ask, Anna held up her hand, "I didn't hear what about, but Josey said they'd discuss it after the party. Richie said something like, 'Please don't tell them' and, well, slunk away. Thinking about it now he looked like a beaten dog. I left quickly before either of them could see me and think I'd been eavesdropping."

"Do you know of anyone else Ms Grace may

have had a falling out with?" Colm asked.

Both women looked thoughtful and then each shook her head. Feeling that they had enough to be going on with, Kate brought the interview to an end. "Thank you for your time and please thank Ms Grey for arranging all this," Kate indicated the debris from their lunches. "I'd like the names and addresses of all the staff involved in Peaceford, please. Artistic and technical."

Anna nodded, "Of course. You can collect that from reception."

The writers stood up and followed Kate and Colm to the door. "I'll take you to the lift," said Suzy, leading the way.

Anna called after them, "I'll let Vanessa on reception know that you need names and addresses."

Suzy left them at the lift and as the doors closed, Colm said, "Did you notice no-one asked why we were asking questions?"

Kate looked thoughtful, "It could just be that Alice's comment about looking at unsolved cases made sense or they might already know about the body. The Super was going to release a report this morning."

Vanessa, the receptionist must have had a personality transplant, Kate concluded. She couldn't have been more helpful and was already printing off the information they needed. She smiled broadly as she handed the sheaf of papers over. "I hope you find out what happened to Josey, Ms Grace," she said. "She was a lovely lady."

Kate stopped in her tracks and turned back to Vanessa. "Did you know Ms Grace well?"

"Well," she flushed a little, "Ms Grace would sometimes come and have a chat with me, if there was a long gap between her scenes."

"That must have brightened your day," said Colm with his winning smile.

"Oh yes. She'd turn up with a cup of tea and say, 'Time for a bit of gossip, Vanny?' That was her nickname for me." There was an increase in the flush that was rising up from her throat.

Kate let Colm take the lead with a subtle nod, and so he asked, "I expect you get to hear all sorts on here?"

Vanessa looked a little coy. "Well, you do sometimes. The phone calls that come through and the meetings over there," she nodded to the little alcove where Kate and Colm had waited earlier. "They sometimes think they can't be heard when they're in there."

"Anything that Ms Grace was interested in?"

Vanessa hesitated, perhaps, belatedly realising that gossiping wasn't the best skill for a receptionist. "Oh, she was interested in everyone. But she never had a bad word to say about anyone. And if I had heard something that could be..." again that hesitation, "difficult for the person concerned, Ms Grace would say she didn't believe it. She always thought well of everyone."

"Yes. She seems to have been a lovely woman," Colm replied.

"She was. I really miss her. I don't believe she just went off. I think something has happened to her. Something bad. I hope you find out what."

"We'll try," Colm reassured her. "Thank you for these print outs." And with that Colm and Kate left.

October 2013

Hello again Sally,

Have you missed me? I've been watching you and just for a while I wondered if you'd taken my first missive to heart and mended your ways. But then I noticed poor Hugh Gifford was no longer your escort of choice and he, poor soul, looked like he had lost something. What secret did you pry out of him? And what has it cost him? And of course there will be more than one payment, won't there, Sally?

Sally Price was a bully. She gathered her sycophants around her but they stayed through fear and everyone avoided being on the wrong side of Sally Price. How did you get into the local high school? You weren't bright enough and yet you won a scholarship. What did you have on whom? Or was it your parents? Was it from them you learnt the art of secrets gathering?

I must confess I have been unable to unravel that particular knot. I think I have all the others. You'd be surprised at the information some people keep; their diaries, their letters. I have them all. They don't make pleasant reading. You see Sally is selfish, egotistical as well as being a bully. And all those flaws were present in her life – weren't they Sally?

I notice Stephen Osborne escorted you to that film night. Is he your next victim? I would be interested to know what you find on him. Or you could leave him alone. Have you realised yet that I have the life and times of Sally Price at my fingertips?
I will write again.

Your Conscience

CHAPTER 13

Back in their car, Kate decided that Hugh Gifford would be their first port of call.

"What about Richie?" asked Colm, "He is known to have had an argument on the day Grace disappeared and he's an ex uni student."

"Well, so am I and so are you. But Richie is going to be either up to his ears trying to undo whatever it is he's got wrong or sulking somewhere because he's just been torn off a strip. No, we'll wait until he's home and, hopefully, more relaxed."

Gifford lived in Hamsworth, on the very edge of Eashire and Kate noticed on their route a sign for Babbington Minor. If she'd been on her own she might have been tempted to take a detour. As it was, they headed straight to Hamsworth.

Gifford's home, Kate decided, was worthy of being called a cottage. Its low walls, small windows and shoulder hugging thatched eaves were all archetypal. Colm stepped and bent forward to knock the door. It was opened promptly by a tall man with a full head of white hair. Kate had thought that since Gifford was playing Grace's husband that he would be of a similar age. In fact he looked to be at least ten years older, if not more.

Both Kate and Colm showed their warrant

cards.

"Ah, police. How interesting. Come in."

He turned and left the door for them to follow and close. He led them into a small room that appeared to have more than its fair share of chairs in all shapes, styles and sizes.

"Please take a seat," he gestured broadly. "Apologies for the excess of choice but I am expecting the local amateur drama group soon, to do a first read through of their autumn play."

Kate and Colm sat on adjacent chairs opposite Hugh Gifford. "I know why you're here," he said as he sat in his own seat. "It was on the local news. You're sure it's her?" But then answered himself. "Of course you are. You wouldn't have released the details if you weren't. Poor Josey!"

"Did you know Ms Grace well?" Kate asked, taking advantage of the opening.

"As well as any of the cast. There is a level of familiarity when one works with the same people time after time."

"Were you friends? You must have had a lot of time together, playing husband and wife."

Gifford shrugged. "Not particularly."

Kate felt there was something just a little too studied about the way Gifford shrugged it off.

"We understand from others that you and she were quite close to start with?"

A slight pause. "I suppose to start with we were. She was new to the show and the area.

She'd left all her close friends in London, so I took her under my wing so to speak."

"Was this a romantic relationship?"

Gifford guffawed. "No, purely platonic. I occasionally escorted her to events, we would have meals together but nothing else."

"So what happened?"

"Happened?" Gifford's reply was a play for time, Kate was sure.

"We were given to understand that you had a falling out," Colm supplied.

Gifford paused. "No. I don't think so. Grace got to know the others better and was no longer reliant on my support. She didn't need my wing, so to speak." He gave a small chuckle.

Kate thought, that even for an actor his words rang false. So she pushed the point, "You never had any falling out or disagreement?"

Gifford shook his head and Kate changed tack.

"Did you attend the show party on the last night Ms Grace was seen?"

"Of course. We all went."

"Did you talk with Ms Grace at all that evening?"

"No, I can't say I did." He looked thoughtful, "You know, in one's memory, childhood summers are always sunny but that evening lived up to those memories. It was a lovely evening and I took a stroll into the garden not long after I arrived, glass in hand. I went beyond where the fairy lights had been trailed and stood in the warm darkness. I looked back at the lights and the gaiety and felt quite nostalgic." He shook himself from his reminiscence. "Not in a morbid way, you know. It was quite a magical evening. Then I heard the chink of someone calling everyone to attention and I noticed a drift towards the conservatory. By the time I'd walked back, Josey was finishing her speech to a polite patter from her audience."

"Did you see anyone else beyond the fairy lights? Further into the garden?"

Gifford was in mid shake of his head when he stopped, "I've just remembered there was someone further in. I couldn't see who it was. In fact, I probably wouldn't have noticed him if he hadn't been smoking. It was the glow of the cigarette end that caught my attention."

"You said 'he'?"

"Could you see who it was?"

"No. Although the moon was out he was stood in the shadows but I could see enough to say it was a big man."

"Big fat or big tall?" Colm asked.

"Definitely tall. Probably about your height, maybe a little larger. Well-built but not fat."

"Did this person also move up to hear Ms Grace's speech?"

Gifford stopped and looked thoughtful but finally offered, "I really can't say. I heard the chink and turned back. I really didn't give this fellow another thought until you started asking me questions."

"Do you think you saw this man at any other time during the evening?"

"No, I don't think so." He shook his head slowly.

"Once Ms Grace's speech was over what did you do?"

"I think I chatted with Chloe and her parents. Chloe was not quite a teenager then, the youngest of our cast. She plays the daughter of the grocer. She didn't appear that often, because of her age. After that I went home."

"What time would that have been, sir?" asked Colm.

"Well, at the time I didn't know but your colleagues provided the details for me. I was picked up by a taxi driver at nine-fifty and he drove me straight home. I arrived home at about ten-fifteen. I changed into my pyjamas, made myself a mug of hot milk and poured myself a stiff whisky. I then sat and listened to the radio until just before midnight."

The last part of his explanation had a rehearsed sound to it but if her colleagues at the time had verified his actions and timings, he'd learnt them off pat. Kate looked across at Colm to see if he had any questions. He closed his notebook and Kate thanked Gifford for his time.

As they were leaving Kate espied three beautiful vases on the dresser in the room. They were wonderful pieces of art and looked a bit like the Moorcroft her mum so liked. "These are beautiful," she said walking towards them. On closer inspection she saw that the designs on them represented the seasons: winter, spring and autumn were there but no summer. "Are you still hunting for the summer one?" she asked.

Gifford shook his head slowly, "No. I know where it is but unfortunately the price to pay is too high."

The phraseology sounded a little strange to Kate's ears but these artistic types; all a bit flowery.

CHAPTER 14

"Do you believe him?" Colm asked as he strapped himself in. "About not falling out with her?"

"No. Something happened but it doesn't seem to have any relevance for us or the night she disappeared."

As Colm drew away, Kate rang in. "Alice, can you check that Hugh Gifford's alibi was checked and verified by the officers back in 2015, please."

There was a pause.

"Thanks, okay. We're off to Stephen Osborne's next. Talk later."

"Mind you, even if they did verify the timings, there's no proof that he didn't go back out and return to Grace's place when everyone else had left."

"True, but do you think he has the physical strength to have moved a dead weight?"

Colm thought, weighing up the question and conceded, "No, even a fit man would find it tough going."

"And how would he get the body from the cottage to the field? He doesn't own a car."

"Right."

"He's not definitely out but he's not a front runner at the moment. Now, let's talk to Stephen Osborne."

Whereas both Grace and Gifford had gone

for old with their homes, Stephen Osborne had opted for new. A detached modern house on an exclusive estate between Eashire and Westergate. The door was opened by a forty-something woman in a sun dress, brushing dirt from her hands as she opened it, "Yes?"

"Mrs Osborne? Is Mr Stephen Osborne at home?" Kate asked as she and Colm showed their identification cards.

"Yes, of course. Come in." She showed them into a bright and light modern room with French doors leading down to the garden.

"Make yourselves comfortable, I'll just go and get him. He's playing with his water feature."

She scurried out through to the garden and Colm raised an eyebrow, "Is that a euphemism?"

"Behave." Kate looked around the room. Photographs of a happy family covered both wall and cabinet space. If this was Stephen Osborne, his looks did not match with her ideas of an actor.

On cue, Stephen Osborne arrived wiping wet hands and forearms with a cloth and showing dirty knees below his shorts. He was a block of a man. In a few years' time, if he wasn't careful, he would be as round as he was tall. Not her idea of an actor at all. And then he spoke.

"Police? I assume this is to do with Josephine Grace and the body you've found?"

Kate introduced them both and marvelled at the sex appeal of this man's voice. It was low, soft and smooth. She wondered if he played a bit of a Casanova on the radio. That voice would allow for such parts.

Mrs Osborne appeared behind her husband, "Can I get you any refreshments? Something cold in this heat?"

"Thank you, that would be lovely."

"Do sit down," she called as she hurried off to get their drinks.

Osborne also sat and looked expectantly at them both. Kate began. "Were you close with Ms Grace?"

"Not particularly."

"We understand that you would escort her to events from time to time, is that so?"

"Oh that!" he waved his ham-like hand. "I only did it on a couple of occasions. I was too vanilla for Josephine Grace." He smiled.

"Vanilla?" Colm queried.

"You know. Nothing exciting, out of the ordinary. No skeletons in the cupboard. Boring, as far as Josey was concerned."

Osborne looked at them. Appraising them, Kate felt. He then seemed to make a decision. "Look, I didn't say this before but since you've found her body I think I should come clean."

Kate and Colm both tensed in their seats.

"I think you should go and have a chat with Craig Masters."

"Who is Craig Masters?"

"Once upon a time he was the actor playing

the temporary vicar in Peaceford but he lost that job."

"How come?" Colm asked.

"Look, I don't know the details but I think you should talk with Craig. It might give you a..." he paused, clearly trying to pick the right word, "...a better understanding of the type of person Josey could be."

"Do you know where we might find this Craig Masters? Is he in Eashire?"

"That I don't know. He was staying above The Mitre in Eastgate but I'm not sure if he's still there or even, as you say, if he's still in Eashire."

Mrs Osborne arrived with a tray of drinks. Cool, homemade lemonade. Once, she handed out the glasses she went and sat on the arm of her husband's chair.

"Did you both attend the show party back in August 2015?" Kate asked.

Mrs Osborne was sipping her drink and just nodded while Stephen said, "Yes. We didn't stop long. Not really our scene. They're all a bit too lovey for us. I'm an ordinary bloke who just happens to have a voice made for radio! I'd never have made it on the box." He laughed as he said this and his wife patted his arm affectionately.

"Do you know what time you left?"

"We think it was about nine forty-five. Give or take a few minutes."

"Did you see Hugh Gifford on your way out?"

"No."

"Yes," contradicted Mrs Osborne. "He was mooching around the front living room and checking out the window. I assumed he was waiting for a taxi."

"And when you got home did either of you go out again?" asked Kate.

"I did," answered Mrs Osborne. "I took the babysitter home. So I was gone about fifteen minutes. Steve had a mug of tea waiting for me when I got back in."

"And neither of you went out again," Kate persisted.

"Nope. Watched a bit of telly and in bed by eleven thirtyish?" Osborne turned to his wife for confirmation and she nodded.

Kate's instincts were telling her that these two were not even in her race let alone front runners. She thanked them for their time and they left. Once the door had closed, Colm confirmed her suspicions, "No, it's not those two."

"Well, we can't rule them out completely, but I agree, they don't sit with what we've got."

February 2014

Hello again, Sally,

Now, why have you taken up with all those youngsters? What can they have that you could use? They're far too young to have done anything interesting. I'm not sure they've even got cupboards, let alone skeletons in them.

But shall we get back to the life story of Sally Price, or rather Melissa Smith! I must say I like the name, Melissa, but Smith! Couldn't you have come up with something a little more original? Now, all the bios on you have the period of '67 to '71 as your lean years: 'jobbing actress' and a bit of shop work. That's not what I've learnt. Melissa Smith was had for soliciting on numerous occasions between summer 1967 and October 1970. I'm sure your fans would be interested to know what kinds of work a 'jobbing actress' took on.

Do you remember Sylvie? Sylvie Hardcastle? She thought you were her best friend. Her diaries for those years are chock full of references to the kindness of Melissa Smith. Sharing pitches so you wouldn't get hurt. Sharing a bedsit to save money. What wonderful, heart-warming times. But she didn't know about the baby selling did she? I read the letter she left for her child. It broke my heart. How much she wanted to keep the child but her best friend, Melissa, said the life chances would be better if the baby was put up for adoption. You didn't tell her about the money did you? And you didn't take her with you when you moved on to better things, did you? Even though those chances were funded by her baby.

Do you know what happened to Sylvie? I don't expect you care, do you? She ended up in an asylum.

Oh, they like to dress it up with fancy words but that's where she spent the last years of her life. She couldn't accept that she'd given away her baby; thank God she didn't know that you'd sold it. She became a menace to new mums and their babies. Taking them. Thinking they were her long lost baby. I was the only one who visited her and that's how I ended up with her diaries. So much torment. And so much of it down to you... Melissa!

It's not too late to change you know. You just have to want to.

Your Conscience

CHAPTER 15

"Craig Masters next?"

"We can give it a go but I don't think he'll still be there after all this time. Is Eastgate on our way to Richie Kershaw's?"

Colm checked the address list and nodded. "Yes. Just a bit of a detour."

In the meantime, Kate called in, "Len? Can you do a check on a Craig Masters, please? Last known address and any background you can pick up."

The Mitre was more or less in the centre of Eastgate, an inter war build of family homes and amenities. Not exactly run down but perhaps on a bit of a slide. The landlady proved to be less than helpful, asserting that they no longer let out rooms and that she'd never heard of Craig Masters. For the time being Kate was happy to let it ride. She'd be back if information gained proved it to be necessary.

Richie Kershaw lived with his mum in a small house on the edge of Eastgate. A cul de sac of identical houses bordered a large green island that gave cars a turning point. Number 52's garden was well tended and in the summer heat the smell of roses wafted in the air. A motorbike was on its stand to the left of the path where the soil had been paved just for the purpose.

A young woman answered the door wearing a pink crop top and very short white shorts. "Yeh?"

"I'm Detective Inspector Medlar. Is Richie Kershaw in?"

The girl turned away and yelled into the gloomy interior, "Mum. It's the police for Richie."

Kate moved into the hallway, following the girl, only to be met by a woman with a scowl that could, as Kate's Mum would have said, curdled butter. "Look, he's a good lad now."

Kate held up a placatory hand, "Mrs Kershaw? Richie's mother? Richie isn't in any trouble as far as I know. We just need to talk with him."

The woman eyed them both suspiciously and then snapped at Colm, "Well shut the door then. Don't want the neighbours knowing my business."

Dutifully, Colm shut the door and the woman called up the stairs, "Richie get down here immediately."

There was several minutes silence and then they all heard the creak of floorboards, the opening and closing of a door and footsteps on the stairs.

"You'd better go in there," the woman indicated the lounge. Although small and the furniture had seen better days, the room was spotlessly clean and family photographs sat proudly on the mantelpiece. Kate noted that the father was not present in these happy snaps. They sat in a chair each. Richie Kershaw followed them in. He was in his late twenties, Kate estimated with a neat musketeer beard and moustache. Light hair was swept back from a broad forehead, which was already seamed with premature worry lines. Dressed in cut off shorts and a T-shirt he looked gangly and still not settled into adult hood.

"Hello, Richie. I'm Detective Inspector Kate Medlar and this is my colleague, Detective Constable Colm Hunter."

Richie nodded. "I know why you're here. I heard it at the station. You've found Josey's body."

"That's right and we need to re-interview everyone who knew her. I understand she was kind to you when you first started at the station?"

"Yeh. Yeh, she was." Kate could hear the 'but'.

"And?"

"No, nothing. She was good to me."

"So would you be surprised to know that someone has reported overhearing an argument between you and Ms Grace on the day of her party?"

Richie's whole body drooped. "So you know what she was going to do?"

Kate thought she would have to play this fish very carefully, "Well, why don't you explain it and we can get your side of the event."

Until now, Mrs Kershaw had been hovering in the door way. Now she came in and sat next to Richie on the sofa. She took his hand and gave it a squeeze. Richie looked at her and she nodded.

Still holding his mother's hand he took a deep breath and exhaled loudly. "Josey was really nice when I first got to know her. Lent me money, showed me the ropes, just talked with me." He paused and looked into the distant past. "So I confided in her. When I was still a kid Dad just upped and left. I didn't take it well and I began to hang around with the wrong kind and got into drugs and violence. You lot," he looked up and briefly met Kate's eye, "caught me and I went to a Young Offenders place."

"And it was the best thing that ever happened to him," interceded Mrs Kershaw.

Richie gave her hand a squeeze and smiled, "Yeh, it was. In there they taught me about recording and stuff and gardening. Me liking gardening," he laughed at himself but then looked sombre. "But I didn't put that bit on my application form when I went for my apprenticeship."

Light dawned for Kate. "So Josey was threatening to tell someone that you had a criminal record?"

Richie nodded miserably. "She said she'd think about it. I promised I'd do anything for her and she said she'd come up with something at the party."

"And did she?" Colm asked.

Richie shook his head. "She refused to acknowledge me at all that evening so in the end I went home." He shrugged. "I thought I'd try and ring her on the Saturday but she didn't pick up and then the police came round and said she'd gone missing."

"That must have been quite a relief for you," Kate thrust.

Richie's head shot up, "I didn't kill her."

"But her disappearing did mean you could forget about the problem."

"No!" said Mrs Kershaw. "Richie got himself into quite a state and he talked it through with me and I said he needed to explain it to his manager."

Richie looked at his mum gratefully, "And I did. He told me I'd been a bloody fool and he checked it with HR and since I was doing well on the scheme they said they would overlook it. Mark did explain I could have been sacked on the spot."

"They said they'd overlook it? Just like that?" There was disbelief in Colm's tone.

Richie flushed, "No, not just like that. I had to go and see Mr Rainsford with Mark and explain why I lied and Mark had to say what I was like in terms of punctuality, work ethic. You know? That sort of thing."

"And he had to wait a week for Mr Rainsford's decision," added Mrs Kershaw.

Kate decided, at least for the time being, that there was little more to gain from talking with Richie Kershaw.

"Thank you for your time, Richie." Kate and Colm stood, "Mrs Kershaw."

Kate nodded her thanks and they left.

CHAPTER 16

Back at the station Colm updated the wall and Kate checked through her emails for any further information. Len had taken the initiative and gone to see Claire Bayntry with photographs of the jewellery. She had been able to positively identify them as Josephine Grace's and that they were her accessories on the night of the party.

"Which proves she must have been killed that night, after the party," Len said.

Kate agreed. Although she'd had little doubt that was the case, the identification of the jewellery just underlined and substantiated the fact. Alice was still compiling names but had managed to come up with a shortlist to start interviewing. Checking her watch, Kate said, "Right, everyone home. We'll start on the interviews fresh in the morning. Len, did you find anything on Craig Masters?"

Len looked up. "I've got a call in to a mate in Bridgewater. I think that's where he is. Should know by tomorrow."

"Great. Come on then. Off you go. We'll meet back here tomorrow, eight o'clock all right for everyone?" Nods and shuffling from her colleagues. Kate tidied her desk as the others got up and left. After Richie's story she was eager to talk with Craig Masters. Perhaps there was more to Josephine Grace than her public knew.

On her way home, Kate stopped off at the little corner shop to pick up food for Monster, a large, hairy, feral, tabby cat, who had adopted her several months ago. She had seen him late March crouching under the hedge between her garden and next door's. He had looked very bedraggled but no amount of persuasion could lure him out. Kate had been unsure, at that stage, whether he was a stray or someone's much beloved pet.

However, the following night he was there again and Kate had felt she must feed him. She put half a can of tuna and a saucer of water under the eaves of the shed where it was driest and called the cat, "Puss! Puss! Puss!" The creature had merely glared at her but an hour later when Kate returned, the dish was empty. And so began her relationship with Monster.

She had tried all her neighbours to find out who Monster belonged to but no-one knew. A chap a few doors up thought he might have belonged to the couple who used to live in number twenty-five, but they'd moved weeks ago. So it seemed like Monster had been abandoned. Not sure of the etiquette with strays, Kate had stopped off at a local vets to ask them what she should do and was dismayed to hear that there was a high probability that if Kate took Monster to a shelter, he would, if not re-homed, be euthanized. So Monster became Kate's responsibility.

Little by little she had moved the feeding dish closer to her back door and then into the kitchen. Reluctantly the cat followed, although the coming into the kitchen took three nights. Very occasionally he would wander into the main room and sit watching Kate with bright amber eyes. Kate had been worried that Monster probably carried a large number of friends. She had once again gone to the vets and acquired a flea and worm treatment that could go in his food. They had suggested that Monster should really be given a once over and, if not already, castrated. Kate wasn't sure she was up to that, yet. Monster still wouldn't allow her to touch him but at least he didn't run away anymore when she was in the kitchen with him.

Now, nearly three months later, as she drove up to her home and parked, Monster was waiting by her gate. He had started doing this about ten days ago and it didn't matter what time she came home. As she climbed out of her car he began to *talk* with her, all the way to the front door. Then, as usual, he disappeared round to the back to wait to be let in through the kitchen.

Having fed Monster, Kate put a meal into the microwave. She knew she ought to cook from fresh more but it seemed so much hassle just for one. Busy making herself a cup of tea as the microwave buzzed away, Kate couldn't help thinking that she'd seen or heard something today that was significant to their understanding of Josephine Grace, but it refused to move to the front of her mind.

Taking her tea through to the lounge, she switched on the television and surfed while waiting the obligatory minute before eating the meal. There was a programme on about Egypt. She was fascinated by this country's history and had promised herself that she would go there, one day. And still something niggled at her mind.

Monster came in and sat alongside the armchair. He ostentatiously washed himself and then sat with his paws curled under him. He was happy to sit in the same room as her and watch and he no longer ran away if she moved out of her seat, but he still wasn't a pet.

Yawning and stretching, Monster, as had become his routine, as though sensing the time, at ten he sat up and walked pointedly towards the back door. It was time for him to go. Kate had no idea where he stayed but was not too concerned, at the moment.

CHAPTER 17

Next morning gathered in the incident room, Kate had formed a plan of campaign. The niggle from last night had coalesced into a positive thought and she now had a hypothesis. One she wanted to try out on her colleagues and one that would need Craig Masters' input.

"Morning all. Len, have you heard back from your mate?"

"No boss, I'll get on to him as soon as we've finished here."

"Okay, I have a theory I want you to think about. The evidence is circumstantial at the moment but it might explain why Josephine Grace was murdered, even if we don't yet know who by."

The others joined Kate at the large central table and took their seats. Kate outlined her conjecture. "Why do we think Grace was going to tell the powers that be that Richie had lied on his application form?" Kate looked round at their faces.

Colm offered, "Because she thought it was wrong to lie?"

"But he wasn't doing any harm, was he?" Alice offered. "And he was proving to be a good apprentice."

"What about blackmail?" suggested Len.

Colm scoffed, "What could Richie give her that she couldn't get for herself?"

"A sense of power? A favour to be repaid in the future?" Kate threw in her own idea.

Colm shook his head, "No. I can't see it."

"What was it Stephen Osborne said about his friendship with Grace? Something about 'no skeletons in his cupboard'?"

Colm flicked through his notes, "Yes. He said he was 'too vanilla'."

"Could that be because Grace couldn't find anything to hold over him?"

Colm still looked doubtful and Kate pushed home her point, "Do you remember what Hugh Gifford said about not having the fourth vase? It was something like 'the price was too high to pay'. Wouldn't somebody say it was 'too expensive' or 'out of my price range'?"

"Actors do tend to talk funny, though, don't they?" Len offered.

"Yes, but I was convinced yesterday that I had seen or heard something significant but I couldn't recall what until the early hours of the morning. I had seen the missing vase from Hugh's collection; summer."

Colm was interested, "Where?"

"In Grace's house. It was on the dresser behind Claire Bayntry's left shoulder when we sat in the kitchen."

Colm followed her reasoning, "So you think Hugh Gifford has a 'skeleton in his cupboard' that our victim found out about and the price for her silence was the vase?"

"Yes. I think probably the first payment at least."

"So, are you going back to Gifford this morning?"

Kate shook her head. "If possible, I want to talk with Craig Masters first. I think Stephen Osborne was pointing us in his direction for a reason."

As if on cue, Len's desk phone rang. Whilst he was answering it, Kate spoke to Alice and Colm, "I'd like you two to start interviewing the cast today. See if you can find others who might have let slip to Grace, things they'd not like out in the open."

Len returned to the table. "That was Bridgewater. Craig Masters is there working in an arts centre." Len passed Kate a slip of paper. "That's the name and number of the DCI in Bridgewater that you should liaise with."

"Thanks Len, that's great. Would you get in touch with the friends that came from London for the party, Gerald Purcell, Raymond Salisbury and Summer Loving. See if they're prepared to come back to Eashire for an interview. It would be easier if they could come here rather than us trekking up to London. Also find out from Claire Bayntry if Grace's solicitor and old friend, Gordon Delver, is due down. I would imagine that he's going to be coming here soon. Again set up an interview; make it tomorrow in business hours."

"Yes boss."

"Okay? I'll give DCI Clifford a call and go and see Craig Masters."

Kate turned to Colm, "Let me know if you find anything interesting."

"Yes boss."

July 2014

Hello again Sally,

Now what did you have on the chap who played the new vicar? I see his contract was short lived. Was that down to you? I'd lay a fiver it was! Wouldn't he play your game? Well, good for him. But you're not learning from my little missives, are you? Listen to Your Conscience before it is too late. You really should. You don't want to meet your maker without making due reparations, do you?

Now, back to the story of Sally Price, aka Melissa Smith. Although Melissa disappeared in 1971, didn't she? I am assuming that it was Sylvie's baby money that set you on your way. And Sylvia was so pathetically grateful that you gave her some money 'from your savings' before leaving. What a hypocrite you are Sally Price.

Now how did John Hatfield find you? I know the official story is he saw you in some amdram but is it just coincidence that his marriage fell apart just after you moved on to a new agent? What barrel did you have him over and did he, in the end, refuse to play your game? It must be something juicy as he has never come out against you. Does he still fear revelations?

I read a piece online, which says that you are sponsoring Summer Loving. Normally I would think, 'what a wonderful thing to do', but I fear your past behaviour makes me ask, 'what will you get out of it?' I shall research. Until next time.

Your Conscience

CHAPTER 18

Heading out of Eashire with the satnav already driving her mad, Kate reflected on the team's reaction to her idea. Not outright rejection but they, being good police officers, wanted the proof. DCI Clifford had suggested that Kate call in the main station and that he would accompany her to interview Masters. He had offered to bring Masters in but Kate wanted him nice and relaxed. She had a feeling he had something delicate to tell them, if her hunch was correct.

Bridgewater Police Centre was easy to find and had plenty of parking space. Kate was envious of their state of the art building. Well, it was certainly more modern than Eashire's was, that was for sure.

DCI Clifford proved to be an affable man. He had a fast receding hair line and had managed the fact with a buzz cut all over. In the morning sunshine it gave his head a frizzy halo. He was a tall man and Kate was worried that he might not get his legs into her car. She'd bought her own and it didn't have quite the leg room of the pool cars. Seeing her vehicle, he grinned and said, "We'll take mine. It's already set for me."

Masters was working at the Parrett Arts Centre. Its outside demeanour showed its industrial past but now colourful banners waved from the windows detailing art classes and exhibitions. Clifford led the way into reception but then stepped back to allow Kate to take charge. The reception desk was empty and Kate rang the bell displayed prominently by a sign that read 'Please ring' and musical notes surrounding it. Kate did as instructed. Where the peal sounded was unknown but they heard nothing in the foyer. But rung it must have because a large, green haired woman came bustling out through a set of double doors. "Hello. Are you the musicians? No, of course you're not." She answered herself without pause.

Clifford and Kate showed their ID cards and Kate asked, "Is Craig Masters in today?"

"Craig? Yes." Her face clearly showed her struggle not to ask what it was about."

Kate merely smiled, "Shall we go and find him?"

The woman shook herself. "Of course. Come this way. He's in the drama studio. Setting up for tonight's music gig." She led the way, talking as she went. "He's a God send. Will turn his hand to anything. He's trying to set up as much as he can because the musicians are late." She finally drew breath outside a set of doors clearly sound proofed. She pulled one of the double doors open and called through, "Craig, there's some police officers to see you," as she led them inside.

It was dim in the studio, apart from a beacon of light to one side where a small, fair haired man, thirty something, was doing something with a sound deck. He looked up as they approached, "Police?"

Kate thought she saw questioning and panic flit across his face. Or it could have been the shadows caused by the sound desk lighting. The woman appeared to be hovering and Clifford turned to her and said, "Thank you. Shall I help you with that door? It looks very heavy." Reluctantly she allowed herself to be led out. Clifford closed the door after her and then stood quietly in the dimness.

Kate turned back to Masters and showed him her ID card, "I'm Detective Inspector Medlar from Eashire and I would like to ask you a few questions. Is here okay?"

"Eashire? "What's this about?"

Kate indicated the rows of chairs put out for that evening's audience. "Shall we sit?"

Masters came out from behind the desk and sat two seats away from Kate, turning his body to face her. "I haven't had anything to do with Eashire for a few years. So I don't know how I can help you."

"I'm investigating the murder of Josephine Grace."

"Josey? You've found her?"

"You knew she'd gone missing?"

"Yeh. I'd already left Eashire when she disappeared but it made all the papers. I didn't know you'd found her body. Where was she?

How did she die?"

"I'm not at liberty to discuss these matters but we have found her and it is clear that she was murdered so we are interviewing everyone who knew her."

"God, you must be scraping the barrel if you've come to me. I only knew her for a few months and that was at least a year before she was..." he stumbled over the word, "...murdered."

"I understand that you and Josey were close at one point. That she took a shine to you."

Kate was sure she saw him wince. "Yes, just for a bit."

Kate played her hunch, "So were the rumours true?"

Masters washed his face with his right hand. "I thought I'd left all this behind me. I don't see what it has to do with Josey being murdered."

"We're just trying to get a better idea of the sort of person Ms Grace was. To some she was lovely, but to others..." Kate left the sentence hanging in mid-air and hoped her silence would force him to reveal the rumour."

He chuckled sardonically. "Yes, Josey was very good at the caring and sharing act. But that's all it was, an act. Once she had your secrets, woe betide you. Then she would hold it over you." He shook his head and stared off. "She said it would be just this one thing but I didn't trust her. There would always be something else. So I said no and she got the rumour mill working and

I lost my job."

"Can you explain the details, please, so that we know it matches our information?"

Masters signed deeply. "It really wasn't anything much but Josey blew it into a sensational exposé and Rainsford said he couldn't take the risk of it not reaching the papers. You see I was playing the vicar in Peaceford. Ironic really given the vicars' reputations today."

Kate pushed for the details and Masters groaned. "I told her it as a bit of a joke. I never dreamt she'd use it against me." He looked at Kate who was still waiting for the details. He took another large breath. "A woman tried to have me charged with indecent exposure. It wasn't!! I got caught short and went behind a bush, what I didn't realise was that this small kid had made a den and I nearly walked over her. She started screaming blue murder and her mother rushed out. Obviously, I tried to put myself tidy but the mother thought I'd been flashing."

"So what happened?"

"She held on to my arm and phoned the police. I did think about running away but I thought it was best to wait and explain. The police took me in and I made a statement. Then I had to wait there for hours while they got statements from the woman and the child. Eventually, I was sent on my way with a telling off from a big wig about urinating in public."

"So how did Ms Grace manage to make that incident cost you your job?"

"Oh, she was very clever. 'I'm sure it's not true but I heard he was a flasher'." He took his voice up several octaves in imitation of a woman. "And it didn't matter that I didn't. Most people's approach was 'no smoke without fire!'"

"Couldn't you appeal?"

Masters scoffed. "My contract was a short one while they tried to see if the character would fit in; they decided he didn't. And to be honest I couldn't cope with all the glances and the conversations that stopped as soon as I walked in. I walked away."

"You left Eashire?"

"Yes, almost immediately. I odd jobbed for quite a few months and then applied for this post about three years ago."

"Where were you on August 15, 2015?"

Masters looked at her blankly. "That's three years ago!"

"Were you working here?"

"Yes. I started in the July. I was probably at a gig." He got up and walked towards the doors, "I'll ask Jan if the archive shows what was on then."

Jan proved helpful and unearthed not only a flier advertising the drama production being shown that evening but also a duty rota. Unfortunately, Masters had not been working that evening.

"Any idea where you were that evening?" Kate asked again.

Masters shrugged. "Do you know what you were doing on August15 three years ago?"

Kate had to concede he had a point but she probably would be able to track back and have some idea. Wouldn't she?

Kate shook Masters' hand, "Thank you for your time, Mr Masters. If you can find a way of confirming where you were on the night in question it would make my life a lot simpler."

Masters nodded and then watched as Kate and Clifford walked away.

"Was it helpful?" Clifford asked as they opened the car doors.

"Yes. I had a theory that our victim was not entirely all that she seemed. Masters has just confirmed that."

"So, you think there were other victims?"

"I'm sure of it. Now I have to find out how many more and who decided they weren't going to put up with her."

"Do you think Masters is a suspect?"

"I think he has to be until we can rule him out."

CHAPTER 19

Colm had won round Vanessa at REAl Radio reception and managed to be allocated a small rehearsal room to conduct their interviews. A fair number of the cast were in today and Colm was happy to interview them as each became free from their recordings. Although he took the lead in questioning, he encouraged Alice to add her own if she thought it appropriate. It was one of Alice's questions with Rosemarie O'Neil, who played the landlady of the Peaceford inn, which opened up that interview.

O'Neil was a fifty something actor who had been in the soap since the start. She and Grace's character had been scripted to have many disagreements; two strong minded women arguing over what was best for people. In real life O'Neil seemed relaxed and easy going. There was a lilt to her voice and the red hair signalled Irish roots. The interview had trundled along its expected route; how long she had known their victim, what she thought of her. Nothing startling came out and then Alice asked, "Did you consider Ms Grace as a friend?"

O'Neil sat up and it was clear that she was giving the question close inspection before she answered. "No. I suppose I didn't trust her."

Colm chimed in, "Trust her, in what way?"

Again O'Neil paused before answering. "I suppose as actors we are always putting on and taking off our characters. With Josey I was never sure that I saw the 'real'..." O'Neil mimed the quotation marks, 'Josey'." Another pause. "I was also a little suspicious about how many friends Josey made and then discarded or, it seemed to me, that they avoided her. Hugh Gifford is a case in point. All over her like a rash and then couldn't bear having to record with her. There was something not right about it."

"But you thought 'the not right' part was Ms Grace not Mr Gifford?"

She nodded. "I've known Hugh for years. He's an easy going sort. Rather old fashioned in his ways but not one to easily take offence. Josey did something that made him very angry. I'm sure of it."

"Did you attend Ms Grace's party on August 15, the night she disappeared?"

"Of course. Everyone connected with the show was there. Josey held court and everyone else milled about. We arrived about eight-thirty, a bit tardy but I'm not a party animal, and we left about ten. Basically just showed our faces."

"We?" Colm queried.

"Yes, my wife!" This was said with some defiance.

"We would like your wife's details so she can corroborate your movements," Colm asked, without a flicker.

"Did you go straight home or stop off anywhere?"

"No, we went straight home."

"Did you drive or taxi?" Alice asked.

"I drove. I don't drink a great deal and apart from half a glass of Champagne when the toasts were given, I didn't have any alcohol."

"So, you got home about what time?" Colm continued.

"Ten-thirty. It's about half an hour from Josey's, although I didn't check the time when we got in. I made a hot drink and Mo had a whisky. We chatted for maybe half an hour, maybe a little longer and then went to bed."

"So neither of you left the house again that evening?"

"No." O'Neil looked at her watch. "I should check where they're up to on the recording schedule. Am I finished here?"

Colm stood up and opened the door for her, "Yes, thank you Ms O'Neil."

CHAPTER 20

Before their next interview, Alice used the contact details for O'Neil's wife to confirm her version of their evening. Coming off the phone she said, "That all tallies. I suppose they have had three years to get their stories straight but she doesn't strike me as the murdering type. I can't see a motive at the moment."

Colm scratched his head, "No, I'm inclined to agree with you but her comments about Gifford were interesting. He made no mention of the fact that he was angry with Grace. Kate will want to follow that up."

"Do you want me to go to the green room and see who's available?"

Colm nodded and Alice disappeared. Within moments she reappeared with a young actor, "This is Tamara Cullen."

She was about mid-twenties and very fragile looking, in a pale interesting way, Colm thought. He gestured to a chair for her and gave one of his winning smiles. "Thank you for coming to speak with us, Ms Cullen."

"Please call me Tamara," her voice was light, a little out of breath as though she'd been rushing.

"Thank you, Tamara it is then. I'm sure you know that we are looking into the disappearance and murder of Josephine Grace?"

Tamara nodded and tears filled her eyes. "She was so lovely to me when I first started." She sniffed, delicately. "She had me go over my lines with her before recordings so I knew what I was saying and she talked about what I was trying to convey beyond the words. She really was very thoughtful." This time the tears flowed. She fumbled in a pocket for a handkerchief and gave a quiet blow. "I really don't know how I can help."

"I'm sorry this is so hard for you but you may, unknowingly, have a vital piece of information, so is it okay to keep going?"

Cullen nodded, if reluctantly. Colm was at a loss as to how to ask the question to support Kate's theory but Alice asked her stock one, "Would you say Ms Grace was a friend?"

"Oh yes. Most definitely."

"So you saw her outside the soap's commitments?" Colm took up the baton.

"Um, well..." Cullen was thinking hard. Too hard? Colm wondered. But then she continued. "At the beginning, when she was giving me so much help, I went to her home a few times but as I found my feet she eased back. You know, allowed me space to make friends with other cast members."

"So, would you say your relationship was more professional?" Alice pushed.

"At the beginning she was very welcoming. She wanted to know all about my family, my background. How I had come to get the part..." She tailed off, looked thoughtful and then looked Colm directly in the eyes. "I hadn't really thought about it before but I think she found me uninteresting. I'd had few experiences and, I suppose, we had little in common."

Colm nodded as though understanding, continuing his questioning. "I assume you went to the show party on the night she disappeared?"

"Oh, yes. Everyone was there, even the techies. She has a beautiful home and it was a lovely summer's evening."

"Can you remember what time you arrived?"

"I think I was one of the first, so about seven fortyish. Josey was in the conservatory with one of her London friends and I went through and said hello. If I'm honest I was a bit uncomfortable because most of the chat was about London and their shared past. About eight, I think, several sets of people came in at the same time and I escaped to chat with Wilf Asquith who plays the postmaster, and his lovely wife, Samira. They'd not long since had a baby and this was their first night out since Angelica had been born. I oohed and aahed over baby photos."

"Did you notice if anyone seemed angry or at odds with Ms Grace?"

"No." She looked thoughtful, trying to recall the events of that evening. "Josey was in the conservatory all evening. I wandered from group to group, chatting. I can't remember anything like that."

"What time did you leave?"

"I'm not sure of the exact time but I got a lift with Wilf and Samira, who said they had to be back for the babysitter by eleven, so I must have been dropped off at about ten to eleven, something like that."

"And did you go out again that evening?"

"No. My flatmate Kay was in and we sat and watched a movie once I'd changed into my pjs."

"Did you ever witness Ms Grace in confrontation with anyone over anything?"

Again a pause and then she shook her head. "I honestly can't think of anyone. Josey seemed well liked by everyone."

Colm glanced towards Alice who gently shook her head, "Thank you Ms... Tamara, you have been very helpful."

Cullen looked between them and then stood. She still had her handkerchief in her hands and Colm noticed that she had been twisting it throughout the interview. Nerves?

As the door closed, Alice said, "She's either very naïve or she's not telling us the whole truth. What do you think?"

Colm looked thoughtful. "Umm. I think there's something there too but we're going to need more information before we can start pumping her. But definitely one I think Kate will want to see."

CHAPTER 21

Kate returned to the station late afternoon. Colm and Alice were still out interviewing Peaceford's cast and Len was plodding through work on his computer. He turned as Kate walked in. "How did it go, boss?"

"I think it supports your idea of blackmail. I'll give the details when the others are back. How have you got on with the victim's London friends?"

"Ah." Len reached for a slip of paper and read, "Mr Delver will be travelling down today and staying at Ms Grace's home and is happy to see you at any point tomorrow. Ms Loving is already here in Eashire, visiting her family, and has volunteered to come into the station later this afternoon." He checked his watch. "In fact she's due in about forty minutes."

"What about Gerald Purcell and Raymond Salisbury?"

"They're both working in London at the moment and can't easily get away. Mr Purcell's agent suggested a video call. I said I'd get back to them once I'd spoken with you."

"Bugger! I'll talk to Bart. I really am not sure about a long distance interview. Can you read their body language in the same way?"

Len shrugged, "Perhaps you could do a first

interview via the video and go and see them if anything interesting turns up?"

Any further discussion was prevented by the return of Alice and Colm. Kate quickly called them all round the table and allowed each of her team to relay the major points from their day's work. "So, Rosemarie O'Neil thinks Grace was untrustworthy and that Gifford was angry with our victim," Kate summarised.

"Yes. And we both think that Tamara Cullen is hiding something."

"But no-one else seems to have a grudge against Grace?"

"Not that they're admitting to."

Kate ran her fingers through her hair, massaging her scalp before issuing her next batch of orders. "Okay. Len arrange a time with Mr Delver for tomorrow and ask Claire Bayntry to also make herself available. Alice, if you could do a financial check on our victim. Not so much what she's worth but any unexpected transactions."

"You're thinking the blackmail price might be more than a few bits of china?" Colm queried.

"It's worth looking into. In the meantime you and I are going to interview Summer Loving in ten minutes. Let's have a quick look at what we've got." Kate waved a manila folder in Colm's direction and he came and sat beside her as they skim-read the information.

Just a little over ten minutes later a

desk phone rang. Alice answered, listened and thanked the person on the other end. She called across as she replaced the receiver, "Summer Loving is downstairs. Garth's put her in the furnished interview room and sounds like he's star struck," she grinned.

Kate returned the grin. "Okay, come on then Colm. I hope you're not going to be the same!"

Colm harrumphed as he followed her out the door.

CHAPTER 22

Kate had to agree that Summer Loving was a stunning looking woman. In magazines you could console yourself that the picture had been airbrushed but in the flesh, she was beautiful. Loving was sat on one of the colourful chairs and smiled at Kate and Colm as they entered.

"Ms Loving, thank you so much for coming in." Kate sat opposite her and Colm sat a little to one side, getting his notebook out.

Loving dismissed Kate's words with a gentle flutter of her hand.

"As you are aware we have found the body of Josephine Grace and ascertained how she died and so this is a murder enquiry."

Loving nodded. Her eyes never left Kate's face.

"Can you tell me a little about your relationship with Ms Grace?"

"Phew!" She slumped a little in her chair and then gathered herself up and began. "I started in Peaceford just before Josey did. I was one of the village children. Everyone was very excited about someone of Josey's calibre being in the show. I didn't know what to expect but Josey was lovely. She talked to everyone and made a point of talking to the three of us who were the voices of all the supposed children."

"So how old were you at this point?" Kate asked.

"Would you believe I was eighteen? But had a very young sounding voice. I'd just finished my A-levels and got a place at drama school so the Peaceford thing was just for the holidays to start with."

"And Ms Grace took an interest in you, how?" asked Kate.

"She was very kind to me and invited me to her home. We watched some of her old performances and she talked me through techniques. Being on the small screen is very different to film and they're both very different to live theatre."

"Would you say your relationship was just professional or a friendship?"

Now, Loving hesitated. Kate didn't know what the calculations were about but she could clearly see them going on behind Loving's eyes. "I suppose more like a mentor. She took an interest in me on a professional level. She even wrote a letter to an agent to ask him to take me on his books. And he did!"

Kate wondered what had been in the letter that made him agree to that. Or perhaps it was just a recommendation. The trouble was the more she found out about Josey, the more cynical she felt.

"I understand you stayed at Ms Grace's home the night of the party? If you have family in

Eashire would you not have stayed with them?"

"Normally, like now, I do but Josey's party coincided with my youngest sister getting married on the Saturday so Mum and Dad's was full of bridesmaids. I was planning to book into the Grand but Josey offered me a spare room."

Were you not a bridesmaid for your sister?" Colm asked, "My sisters would kill me if they weren't bridesmaids at my wedding."

Loving laughed. "April and I had a long chat about how important it was for it to be her day and we both felt that if I was there as a bridesmaid it would ruin it for her."

"Oh paparazzi!" Colm said with dawning understanding.

Loving smiled and Kate intervened, "Did you talk with Josey at all at the party?"

Loving blushed, "Well of course I spoke with her but it was light chit chat, suitable for a party. Nothing of significance."

"What time did you retire that evening?"

Loving looked down to the carpet and shook her head. "I don't know the exact time. There were still guests there but I was shattered."

"Who was still there when you retired?"

Loving looked thoughtful and then spoke, ticking names off on her fingers as she went. Gerald Purcell and Richard Salisbury were trying to sort out a taxi that hadn't turned up and then there was..." she paused, "Isn't it terrible? It's only been three years but I can't remember their names. They left Peaceford shortly after Josey went missing and got married, I think."

Kate was convinced Loving was lying but what about? Did Loving have a guilty secret? That could be disastrous for a rising star. How convenient then if the source of your worry disappears. But she couldn't see Loving as a murderer but what was she lying about?

Getting up to leave, Loving suddenly clicked her fingers, "Can't remember her name but he was called Watters, I think. No, I'm sure. Watters."

Having nothing further to ask at this stage, Kate thanked Loving for coming in and left Colm to see the star out of the station.

CHAPTER 23

As soon as Kate entered the incident room both Len and Alice turned in her direction. Kate nodded to Len first. "Mr Delver will be available from nine tomorrow morning and Ms Bayntry says she will also be available."

"Thanks Len." Turning to Alice, "Alice?"

"I've managed to get hold of her bank statements etc. She's not a particularly wealthy woman. The house appears to be her only asset. However, she has a monthly amount from REAl Radio and then another two payments of similar amounts from unknown sources. I'm trying to track them back now."

"Possibly blackmail money?" Len offered.

"Perhaps," Alice agreed," but the other interesting thing is that some months, apart from her direct debits, she doesn't withdraw any money at all. Not for shopping or anything else!"

"Could others of her victims be paying in cash?" Kate mused. "I wonder how much Ms Bayntry knew about her employer's side-line? Anything else?" She looked from one to the other. Right, I'm going to go and have a chat with Bart about our London interviews."

Bart was quite adamant, "Go and see them in person, Kate. If our victim had something on them, you need to meet and gauge body language. I don't think that's as clear on these video calls."

Kate nodded. Bart was echoing her own concerns. Some of the younger staff might think it a bit of a dinosaur attitude but she liked to be able to see the whites of their eyes and the crossing of their legs!

Back in the room, Kate called across to Len, "Please arrange times to interview Purcell and Salisbury on Saturday to coincide with train times from here to London. And would you book two tickets for a train leaving Eashire about seven-thirty on that day?"

"On it," Len raised a hand.

At that moment, Colm entered the room, "Who's off to the big city and the bright lights?"

"We are. I'll show you the sights!" smiled Kate.

"Saturday?" Colm questioned.

Kate turned to look at him properly. It wasn't like Colm to quibble over weekend working, especially on an active case. "Is that a problem? I can take Alice or Len, if you prefer."

"No. No. Not a problem," Colm smiled. "I'll look forward to it."

Kate nodded, convinced that something was the matter but Colm clearly didn't want to discuss it. "Right, tomorrow. Colm, how many more cast members are still on your list?"

"Only half a dozen or so but they're not recording tomorrow so do you want me to leave it until Monday or track them down over the weekend?"

"What about the technicians?"

"They're a bit more difficult to get hold of in work because they're working. We did manage to talk with Mark Highfield, Richie's boss and confirmed his story as well as ascertaining if our victim had anything on him. He seems to be in the clear."

"We also spoke to a couple of the studio sparks," Alice chimed in, "but they didn't really know the cast and only went to the party because there was free alcohol and food on the go!"

Kate shrugged, "Fair enough. Okay, tomorrow. Colm you and I will go and see Mr Gordon Delver at the victim's home. Hopefully, we can have a look at the will, see if that holds any surprises. We'll also have another chat with the PA. I'm sure she's not telling the whole truth."

"You don't think she did her own boss in?"

"Might be, depends who Grace left her estate to. But no. I don't think she's our murderer but she is definitely not telling us something. After that I want to have another chat with Gifford, about his anger and his summer vase."

Colm nodded, making notes as Kate talked. "Alice, if you and Len could divvy up the following activities. See if you can track down those unexpected deposits. Give me some background on Purcell and Salisbury, in particular how and when they knew Grace. Also, search for rumours of possible secrets about the pair of them. And see if you can find a Mr Watters from the cast of Peaceford and a woman who left at the same time as he did, possibly now married." Kate turned back to Colm but he had stepped outside with his mobile. Kate wondered if he was having to cancel an arrangement for Saturday. Well, he'd tell her in his own good time if he felt she needed to know.

"But for now, I think it's time to go home." This case did not have the urgency of a fresh kill and in three years there had been no other obvious victims. There was no sense in exhausting people on this one, yet.

CHAPTER 24

Kate had woken early with the case and her ideas running amok. She decided if she was awake she may as well go to the gym and see if Jude was working. Just before leaving the house she texted Colm to meet her at Grace's house at nine. That would give her time to have a good workout, shower and breakfast before the day started properly.

On first entering the equipment room there was no sign of Jude. Kate wouldn't listen to the voice of disappointment. She started with the cycling machine; programming a gentle, flat ride until her muscles had warmed and stretched a little. Then she went for a more hilly ride. Not exactly mountainous but no walk in the park either. She was just warming down when she noticed Jude enter the room and head her way. She waited until Kate had finished before speaking.

"Morning. I thought the early starts had become too much," she grinned.

Kate answered the grin, "No, it's work that has become too much. So I made a point of getting here this morning."

Jude was not exactly hopping from foot to foot but there was something that gave off agitation vibes. "I enjoyed our drink the other evening."

"Me too," Kate said sincerely.

"Did you mean what you said about trying Bridgewater's scene at some point?"

Kate dismounted and used the cloth and cleaning fluid to wipe down her machine before she towelled herself. "Yes. I'd love to. Before I get too old!"

Jude's grin broadened, "A group of us are going this Saturday, if you'd like to come."

Kate's heart sank, "I'm probably not going to be able to make it."

"Oh, okay. Just a thought." And Jude went to move away.

Instinctively, Kate grabbed her arm, "Look, I really would like to go, honest, but my case is taking me to London on Saturday and I'm not sure what time I'll be back."

Jude turned back and appraised Kate carefully. So much so that Kate felt forced to say, whilst doing the action, "Cut me throat and hope to die!"

Jude laughed, her face open and sunny again. "Look, we were planning to meet up at the Crown and Gown, do you know it?"

Kate nodded and Jude continued. "We're meeting at seven-thirty and planning to get a taxi at eight. If you're back in time, meet us there. If not, we'll arrange another time. Okay?"

"Great. I will try and make it." Kate took another breath and asked, "May I have your mobile number and then I can text and let you know rather than you and your friends just hanging around?"

"Yes sure." They exchanged numbers and then Jude said, "Right, I see that Elaine has arrived." Jude turned away and called over her shoulder, "Hopefully see you Saturday."

"Yes, sure. If I can." Kate moved to the weights. She didn't do many and was not into how many kilos she could lift. It was just enough to keep her arms and shoulders toned. Whilst squatting and pushing, she let her mind wander to Jude's offer. Not exactly a date if there were going to be others there. Perhaps one of the others is her partner. She hadn't thought about that. Perhaps Jude was just being friendly and she was misreading all the signs. She'd been out of the game too long. She and Robyn had been together just over two years until she walked out nearly a year ago. Three years since she'd had to do the singles thing. Perhaps she was too old for the game.

Finishing the weights she checked her watch and headed sharply for the showers, all thoughts of nights out pushed to the back while her mind began to tussle again with the character of Josephine Grace and her murder.

CHAPTER 25

Colm was already waiting outside his car when Kate drew up. He smiled and gave a little finger wave as she parked behind his vehicle. He hadn't gone onto the driveway but parked in the road. Two vehicles already occupied the gravel. One was a small Fiat Panda, pale blue with a three year old plate and the other was a BMW 3 Series, dark, almost midnight blue with last year's plate. Kate made a guess at the Fiat belonging to Claire Bayntry, the PA and the BMW to the solicitor, Gordon Delver.

They crunched noisily to the front door and rang the bell. Once again Kate noted that the door furniture was immaculate. The door swung open and Clair Bayntry stepped back to allow them both to enter. "Gordon is in the conservatory. I'll take you through."

They followed her into the room opposite the kitchen, leading into a conservatory that extended along the length of the house. Kate saw the kitchen entrance that she had used last time they were here.

Gordon Delver was your typical solicitor in a dark three piece suit, dark tie with a white shirt and the peak of a white handkerchief in his breast pocket. The black and white effect was enhanced by the white of his hair and the dark of his eyebrows. The eyes beneath them were alert and scrutinised them both as he shook their hands. Kate estimated his age to be well over seventy.

"Detective Inspector Medlar. Detective Constable Hunter." He waved them to a two-seater sofa and sat himself in the chair he had recently vacated. "Medlar. That's an unusual name. Is it the fruit or the person?"

Kate smiled, "It's the fruit."

Claire Bayntry interrupted, "May I get anyone a drink? Tea? Coffee?"

Nobody wanted anything and she left saying, "I'll be in the kitchen when you wish to speak with me." She carefully closed the French doors behind her and a few minutes later Kate heard the kitchen one being closed as well.

Delver rubbed his hands together, "I am assuming you would like to know what is in Josey's will? I am both her legal representative and an executor of the will."

Kate nodded and Delver continued. "Josey lodged a copy of her will with my office and had a copy here, in her study. I checked the one here to ensure that it was the same as the one I held. Clients have been known to make wills and forget to inform the holders of another will. I didn't think this likely in Josey's case but I checked to be sure."

"And were they the same?" asked Colm.

"Oh yes, yes. However, the envelope

contained something, or more specifically 'things', that were not in the envelope of the copy I held. I believe they may have some bearing on your case." With a little flourish he produced five or six pages of writing. The pages were torn from a spiral bound notepad, the rough edges still there. The writing was careful. Letters of a similar size and space. A very regular writing style.

"I'll give you time to read through them. It won't take you long."

Kate quickly placed each sheet in its own evidence bag and then scanned the letters until she came to the last:

July 2015

Hello Sally,

Have you truly mended your ways? I see no outward sign of more victims but that's always been your style, hasn't it? A beautiful façade masking a rotten interior. So I need you to show me that you have changed your ways. That you truly seek forgiveness. So when you give your fancy party next month I want you to announce your retirement.

If you don't then I shall take it as a sign that you are beyond redemption and that you will meet your maker with your sins upon your heart. I shall know, Sally and I shall act.

Your Conscience

"Have you read these letters, Mr Delver? Do you know if the contents are accurate?"

Delver bowed his head. "I have read them. I am at a quandary whether to believe them or not. It is not the Josey Grace I knew and I have known her for more than thirty years."

Colm waved the wad of papers now in his hands, "There's no specific threat here. Even the last one doesn't actually say I will kill you, does it?"

"No, but it does give us an unknown suspect that was not pleased with the way he perceived she ran her life."

Delver coughed, slightly embarrassed, "Is what they say true?"

Kate could see confusion and wariness in his eyes, "We don't know about the historical stuff but we do have testimony from someone who believed Ms Grace was trying to blackmail him."

"And lived to regret it when he refused," added Colm.

"And we are following up on some other matters, which may also confirm the suggestions in these letters."

Delver slumped back in the chair, his professional façade absent, just for a moment. Kate sensed that his idol had been toppled.

"Did these come with envelopes? Do you

know?"

Delver shook his head, still slumped in the chair. "No, they were as you have them now, slotted in the same envelope as her will."

"Do you think she deliberately put them there, to be found if she died?"

"Knowing Josey," he gave a mirthless chuckle, "although it appears to me I didn't know her at all. But I would think that leaving them with her will was a deliberate act."

Kate saw that Delver's hand trembled as he lifted a hand to his brow. To find out that someone you have considered a friend for the last thirty years was not the person you thought you knew had obviously hit him hard. With a conscious effort, Delver pushed himself out of his seat. "Will you excuse me for a moment, I just…" he tailed off.

"Take your time, sir," Kate called after his departing figure.

Once the door had closed again, Colm said, "Poor sod. He looks like his whole world has just imploded."

Kate agreed, "I wonder why she didn't destroy them?" nodding at the letters still in Colm's hand. "They're quite incriminating, aren't they? Both about her past and her present activities."

"Do you think she was in fear of her life and thought she would leave us clues?"

"Possibly. Or were they just there, where no-one would think to look, until she had made up her mind what she was going to do?"

"It's a bugger the envelopes aren't with them."

"Assuming they had envelopes. They may have been delivered just as folded notes." Kate was thoughtful and then contradicted herself. "No, there would have had envelopes. Our writer wouldn't want anyone else reading these."

"Perhaps the PA knows about them."

"Yes, we'll ask her."

CHAPTER 26

The door opened and Mr Delver returned. Kaye noticed that the handkerchief was no longer present in his breast pocket and that his nose was a little redder. Delver looked a little embarrassed, "My apologies, I'm afraid my emotions got the better of me." He returned to his seat, "Now what else may I help you with?"

"Is there anything in her will that is pertinent to her death, do you think?" Kate asked specifically.

Delver shook his head, "I don't think so. Claire, Ms Bayntry, gets a reasonable lump sum and the gardener a small bequest but everything else is to be sold off and invested to create the Josey Grace Scholarship for the Performing Arts."

"And will that be a significant amount?"

"I think with careful investment it could achieve about ten thousand a year."

Colm whistled, "Not to be sneezed at if you're a penniless student."

Delver nodded wisely, "Indeed."

Kate was frustrated. Letters that could be from their murderer but no way of knowing how their victim received them and the will gave no indication of motive either. The letter writer had motive if he, mind you letter writers were often female, they, were outraged by her behaviour, past and present. Was it someone from Grace's past? Why had Sylvie Hardcastle warranted particular mention? Was it because of the selling of her baby? Was that what had outraged the writer? More questions and no answers.

Colm filled the space created by Kate's musings, "What's the name of the gardener? He must have worked a while for Ms Grace if he too receives a bequest."

"His name is Will Miller. I don't think it's William. He came to work for Josey about seven, maybe eight years ago. He keeps the garden pristine, of course, but he also does handyman tasks around the place as well. Josey always said he was worth his weight in gold."

Kate drew herself back to the interview. "You said you had known Ms Grace for thirty years or so. How did that come about?"

Delver straightened himself in his seat. "I first met Josey when she was divorcing her first husband and then she came to me again about another matter and a friendship grew. Josey wasn't one for office meetings. If you needed to have a meeting with her you found a nice café or tea shop. Then she kindly sent me and my wife tickets for an opening night and Josey and Kitty hit it off straight away. I suppose in many ways much of the friendship was between the two women."

"Was your wife still friends with Josey. I noticed that she wasn't on the guest list for

Josey's party?"

Delver smiled wistfully, "Unfortunately my dear Kitty died six years and three months ago. Cancer."

"I am sorry," Kate offered.

Delver waved the commiseration aside, "You hear people say 'it was a blessing when they died', but it really was in this case. I miss her but I prefer that to knowing she was languishing in constant pain."

Kate could understand that sentiment. She moved on with her questioning. "What time did you arrive on the night of Josey's party in August 2015?"

Delver sat back, steepled his fingers with his elbows resting on the chair arms. "I came straight from work, although I left early, three o'clock to catch the 16:04. I'd already got my overnight bag with me. I arrived on time, which was about twenty past six. I got a taxi to the house and had time to wash and change ready for the first guest's arrival just after seven-thirty."

"Who was the first guest?" Colm asked.

Delver looked a little bashful, "I didn't really see. I was on my way to the kitchen to find food. I'd only managed a sandwich on the train and I was hungry. I believe it was Purcell and Salisbury. I know when I went into the conservatory twenty minutes or so later they were there."

"Had they also travelled down by train? Did you see them?"

"I expect they did but they would have travelled first class. A luxury I don't indulge in for myself." He smiled benignly.

"Did you notice anything or anyone amiss that evening?" Kate pressed on.

"No, it was a lovely evening. I spoke to a few people but I didn't really know anyone, apart from Claire, and she was busy making sure everything went well."

"We understand you retired to your room before the party ended?"

"Yes. At my age those kind of gatherings have a limited fascination. Once Josey had given her speech I took the opportunity of whispering that I was off to bed. She smiled, patted my hand and said, 'We'll talk tomorrow, Gordon, darling.'" He stopped and reached into his trouser pocket for his handkerchief and dabbed at his eyes. "Those were the last words she ever said to me."

"Do you think there was anything specific when she said you'd talk tomorrow?"

Delver looked thoughtful, "We did have some client things to discuss and perhaps, in the light of those letters, she did mean more but I didn't pick up on anything as I said my goodnight."

"Were you aware of the party once you'd retired. I imagine it must have been quite noisy."

"To be honest, it was rather pleasant. I sat in my room and read for a while and the music and quiet chatter were a mere background melody!"

"Were you aware of the party ending?"

"No, not really. About eleven-thirty I climbed into bed and slept."

"And you didn't hear anything else that night?"

Delver paused, "Actually I did. I heard a slamming door. It sounded quite close so I thought it was Ms Loving. Her room was next to mine."

"What time was that?"

"I don't know. I was faced away from my clock and too comfortable to turn to look. It didn't feel very late, if you know what I mean. I didn't think it was the middle of the night."

Interesting. She had been sure Loving had been lying about something. Perhaps she had talked to their victim and had a screaming row. Lost her temper and... It was another hypothesis.

Kate looked to Colm who was returning his notebook to his pocket. She too thought they had enough to be going on with.

"Are you stopping in Eashire for long, Mr Delver?"

"I am here for a few days to sort through paperwork and then I will need to return to my office but I am at your convenience whenever you need."

"Thank you, sir." They all rose and Delver shook their hands again. As they were leaving, Delver said, "Even if those letters contain some truth, I hope you find whoever murdered Josey."

"We will certainly try, sir," Kate acknowledged.

CHAPTER 27

Claire Bayntry was sat at the kitchen table, reading. As Kate and Colm entered she looked up and removed her glasses. "Can I get you any refreshments?"

Kate smiled but said, "No, thank you. Hopefully we won't take up too much of your time." As though only just noticing it, Kate stepped over to the dresser, "What a lovely vase. Doesn't Mr Gifford have something similar?"

Claire turned round and smiled broadly, "He does and that was a gift to Josey from Hugh. So generous of him. But that's the sort of behaviour Josey inspired. This house is full of knickknacks from friends and colleagues."

Colm raised an eyebrow but made no comment.

Kate took a seat next to him and began, "Mr Delver seems sure he heard a noise in the night that woke him." She didn't specify when or what that noise was. "Did you hear anything?"

Bayntry looked uncomfortable and her fingers played with her glasses absently. Kate pressed her a little, "I got the impression when we spoke earlier that you may have heard a noise but thought it wasn't relevant. Can I just say, everything is relevant to us. It is our job to rule something in or out."

Still, Bayntry fiddled. Finally, she looked up. "I may have heard something but I wasn't sure what and then there was nothing else so I just turned over and went back to sleep."

"Do you know what sort of time that was?"

Kate was sure that Bayntry was making calculations. What time had Delver said? Should she admit to knowing the time? Would it look suspicious if she said she didn't know? Most people look at their clock if they're woken from sleep.

"It was two-fifteen. I thought it a little late for Josey to still be up but thought I must have heard her coming to bed. As I said there were no further noises so I went back to sleep." All the time she was talking Bayntry was avoiding eye contact and looking over Kate's shoulder.

Kate was sure she was lying, but what about? The time or that she did investigate? "You didn't hear any further noises of Ms Grace getting ready for bed? Wouldn't you normally?"

"I... er... assumed it was Josey closing her en-suite door that had woken me and that she was now in bed." Still no eye contact.

"Did Ms Summer drive to Eashire?" Kate hoped the change of direction might unsettle their witness because there was definitely something she wasn't telling. Kate just knew it. Intuition, copper's nose. Call it what you will, she had that feeling.

"Er... yes." Clearly surprised by the change.

"Did she park on the drive?"

"No. She parked up in front of the garage so it left the drive free for other guests."

"And was it still in the same place when she left the following morning?"

Bayntry paused and then nodded, "Yes, I think so."

"You said before that if Ms Grace had ordered a taxi you would have heard it on the gravel. Would any vehicle coming on to the drive wake you?"

"Oh yes. I'm a very light sleeper." The answer convinced Kate that she had heard something more on the night of their victim's disappearance.

"And yet you didn't hear anything other than what might have been Ms Grace coming to bed?" Kate deliberately allowed her disbelief to leak through.

"No." Bayntry bit her lip and Kate wondered if subconsciously she was preventing her mouth from telling the truth. Okay, she'd leave it for now but she'd be back.

Now, Kate moved on, "Mr Delver has found these letters in with Ms Grace's will." Kate held up the small collection, now in plastic bags. "Have you seen them before?"

Bayntry stared at them and shook her head.

"Did you deal with all Ms Grace's mail?" Colm asked.

Again, Bayntry shook her head. "Obvious

bills I dealt with but letters that looked like fan members or private I put to one side for Josey to deal with. She was very particular about reading and answering fan mail."

"So, she answered all her own fan mail? That must have been quite a task."

Bayntry carefully explained. "Josey would read the letter and then mark on it some comment or other that I would then feed in to a sort of proforma letter. She wanted it to be a little more individual."

"Did she get a lot of fan mail or private mail?"

"Not as much as she used to but she always had set aside time to do her letters. Even when she was getting sack loads. And of course she also received letters at the radio studio."

No joy about when and how the letters arrived, Kate thought, or even if they'd been delivered to the house.

"Thank you for your time Ms Bayntry." Bayntry went to rise and Kate continued, "Is the gardener working today?"

"Will. Umm, yes. I think he's in his workshop. Shall I go and get him?"

"If you wouldn't mind. Thank you." Bayntry left with a sense of relief.

"Did you think that Loving had argued with Josey, killed her and then used her car?" Colm asked.

"It's a possible scenario but I am convinced that both Claire Bayntry and Summer Loving are telling us edited versions of the truth. And I want the truth and I want to know why."

CHAPTER 28

Will Miller was a giant of a man. Kate could see that he was taller than Colm's six foot two and broader. He looked to be in his early forties with light hair bleached white in places by the sun. His forearms were like telegraph poles and were brown with golden hairs. He was wearing old jeans with rips that had been made from use not from fashion and a T-shirt that stretched revealingly across a well-toned torso. His hands were like shovels and even Colm's looked lost in his grip as he shook hands. "I understand you wish to speak with me?"

"Thank you, yes. Please sit down."

Claire Bayntry had not returned with Will Miller and Kate was pleased about her sensibilities. Kate was sure she heard the chair creak under Will but he sat down and leaned back with his legs stretched under the table and his arms on top of it.

"I don't know if Ms Bayntry has told you but we have found the body of Ms Grace and are looking into her murder."

"Yes, she told me," he shook his head sadly, "I really had hoped she'd just gone away."

"Did you talk with Ms Grace very often?"

He looked thoughtful. "Not that often. Normally, if something specific needed doing,

Claire, Ms Bayntry would let me know. Sometimes Ms Grace would come into the garden when I was working and talk about some of the plants." He laughed gently, "She didn't know a lot about plants but she asked intelligent questions."

"When did you start working for Ms Grace?"

"Oh blimey," he rubbed his chin, "I think it was spring 2010." He nodded with more confidence, "Yes, spring 2010."

"Where had you been working before?" Colm asked. "Jobs like this, in this day and age, must be hard to come by?"

"Yes, you're right. I had worked in a lot of jobs, handyman, gardener. For a short time I worked in London tending parks but austerity cuts lost me that one."

Kate was intrigued, "So what brought you from London to Eashire?"

"A string of jobs really. I tried to go where the work was. Who was it said we had to get on our bikes? Was that Thatcher?"

"So, how did you find out about the job here?"

He rubbed his face, hiding his eyes briefly. Once again Kate had that tingling feeling. "To be honest I read an article in a magazine about Ms Grace and her new home and it was obvious that the garden was a mess. You wouldn't think so now but the previous owners had really let it drift back to nature."

Kate waited. They still didn't have a proper answer. Taking his cue, Miller continued. "I sent her a little missive saying that I was a keen gardener and that I could also turn my hand to most household repairs and would she consider me for the post if she was thinking about employing someone."

"And she did." Colm finished. "Just like that?"

Miller grinned. "Oh no. Ms Grace was a shrewd woman. She made me go and have an interview with Mr Delver and then another one here. I was then given a six month trial period. It was an ideal time for me in the garden and I soon began to make inroads. Ms Grace was pleased and made me permanent."

"Do you live in?" Kate asked.

"Oh. No. I have a little house on the road back into Eashire. Nothing grand but it serves me fine."

"Have you always lived there?"

"No, I rented for a few months until Ms Grace made me permanent and then bought."

"I hope you don't mind me asking but I can't see your job paying very well. How do you afford the mortgage?"

Miller blushed. "Firstly, I can turn my hand to anything. So I pick up work from all over."

"But a mortgage company isn't going to accept that. So how did you manage to buy?" Kate persisted.

"I have always lived frugally and the house was virtually derelict when I bought it, for cash, five thousand pounds! It's taken me until now to complete the last job, which was dry lining the cellar."

"Good for you," said Colm, with genuine admiration.

Miller reached into his back pocket and pulled out a phone. "I've kept a record. You know before and after." He fiddled with the buttons and then passed it over to Colm, "That's what it looked like when I bought it."

Kate looked over and saw a derelict cottage. Half a roof and windowless. "You lived there when it was like that?" Incredulity raising the pitch of her voice.

"Had to. Couldn't afford to mend and rent. I made a dry spot in the dining room come kitchen and worked out of that for three years!"

"But what about all the specialist jobs?" Colm asked, clearly intrigued.

Miller grinned, "You can learn just about anything on the internet and most house jobs have got videos as well. It's amazing what you can learn and what you can bodge if you have to."

Colm handed the phone back, having swiped through a few pictures of the cottage's renovations. Taking it, Miller asked, "Is that everything?"

"One last thing," Kate added, "were you here on the night of the party?"

Miller shook his head. "No, I worked in the garden, tidying up, helping the lighting guys and left about six. I came back in at nine the following morning and about ten I saw Mr Delver and Claire searching the garden for Ms Grace."

"Had you spoken with her the day she disappeared?"

"No. Claire gave me all the information about the party and it was down to me to check that everything was okay. And it was."

"Thank you for your time, Mr Miller." With that he eased himself out of the chair and left via the French doors. Kate looked thoughtfully after him.

CHAPTER 29

Colm waited until they were in the car before trying to make the pieces fit their puzzle. "She's still not telling us the truth, is she? She definitely heard something. But was it the same noise as the solicitor heard? Two fifteen seems a little late according to Delver. He thought it was earlier."

"He could have been wrong about the time. He didn't check."

"Maybe the PA even went to investigate. She could have seen something. But what does she get out of an undiscovered murder?"

Kate shrugged, "I agree, she's holding something back, but I can't see her as the murderer. There again she's had a nice life these last three years; living in our victim's home, presumably still being paid her wages."

"So, actually a murder without a body was very helpful to her!"

"Yes. But how did she get the body to that field? How did she know about the preservation order on the trees? And how did she get that fungus thing Gus told us about?"

Kate shook her head. They were getting more pieces but still finding more questions. "I'm going to give Mike a ring and see if it's worth dropping these off," waving the six evidence bags, "before we go and see Hugh Gifford."

"Isn't Bagshaw bringing in his person of interest today? Might be a lot of forensics."

Kate thought the same, which was why she was ringing. Unfortunately, Bagshaw's case had hit the forensics team like a tsunami.

"Bagshaw's dropped off a van's worth of forensics that will keep us going for a decade," Mike said when he realised what Kate wanted. "Look, tell you what. Drop it in before the end of play today and I'll try and get a look at it over the weekend. Probably Sunday."

"Thanks, Mike. I owe you."

"Not as much as Bagshaw will!" Mike laughed as he hung up.

Having picked up the gist of the conversation, Colm switched on the engine, "Gifford's place then?"

Kate nodded. "Let's see if he'll come clean about whatever it was Josey had on him."

Kate rang the doorbell but there was no reply. She tried again. She was just about to give up when they heard the tap of a cane on stone and Hugh Gifford appeared from around the side of the house, dressed in a white linen suit and a Panama hat. "Ah. Di Medley and her colleague. Come this way." He turned and headed down the side of the cottage talking over his shoulder as he went. "It's not often that the days are warm enough for me to sit out but today is ideal. Do come and sit."

The garden they stepped into was simple in

design. A central path through a mown lawn with flower beds running the length of each of them. On one side a gazebo had been set up with one side up providing a shady area. Gifford's seat was on the edge of the shade and he moved it further into the sun before he sat down.

Pointing at a small building, possibly the coal shed in times gone by, he told Colm, "There are chairs in there, fetch yourself a pair."

Colm wandered off and Kate admired the garden. "Do you look after this yourself?"

Gifford laughed. "No, my dear. My wife always told me to stay clear. She did it all, right up to her death and now my dear son and his wife come in once a fortnight and do a tidy for me. They're very good to me."

Kate nodded and watched as Colm snapped two director's chairs into shape and placed them in the shade. Once settled Kate looked directly at Gifford, who had been watching both of them somewhat pensively. She began. "Mr Gifford we have conducted a large number of interviews since we last spoke with you and we have been told that you were angry with Ms Grace rather than her no longer 'needing your wing'."

"Well, I don't know who would say that about me."

"Is it true?"

"I don't tend to get angry very easily, you know."

"No, but she had done something quite

outrageous hadn't she?"

Until that point Gifford had been staring at the tip of his cane, which he'd wedged between his knees, now he looked up. Then he began to nod, "You know, don't you?"

"I could make an educated guess having seen your summer vase in Ms Grace's kitchen."

Gifford grimaced. "That collection was my pride and joy, which was why, of course, she made me give her one of them."

"Did she ask for money as well?" asked Colm.

Gifford nodded. "Every so often I would receive a call from her. Anyone listening in would have thought it was just general chitchat but somewhere in the conversation she would slip in how much she wanted that month."

"Was that every month?"

"Oh no. She knew I had other responsibilities and so it would be once in a while. Which, in a way made it worse because you never knew when it was going to come." Tears filled his eyes and he looked away.

"Can you tell us what she was blackmailing you about?"

Gifford breathed heavily. "Will this need to go any further?"

"Unless it is pertinent to Ms Grace's death, then no."

"Oh, I didn't kill her. I might have wished her dead but I am too much of a coward to actually do anything about it. That was how come she could so easily blackmail me." He looked across his garden and began, "My wife and I knew each other from our school days. She was two years below me. You never could meet a sunnier or more kind person in your life. She lit up my world. I fell for her and, I am surprised to say, she reciprocated." A smile played around his lips as he watched his past self. "I was off to a London college to do performing arts and it was our last night together and," he coughed a little, clearly embarrassed, "well one thing led to another and we consummated our love."

Kate smiled encouragingly, "Unfortunately, Rachel was still under age. Not something that concerned us at the time but Rachel's father found out and threatened to go to the police. I don't know what Rachel said to dissuade him but after three weeks of it hanging over us he relented." He paused. "I can't remember how it came out in a conversation Josey, Rachel and I were having one evening. I suppose fifty years later we couldn't see it having any consequences but Josey squirrelled it away and then..." He drifted off. "When she mentioned it next it had become something sordid. And I knew she would start a whispering campaign. Well you know the rest."

"What did your wife say?"

"I never told her. She would have worried herself to death about it. It was her only fault – she was a worry wart."

"Do you know of any other people Ms Grace may have done the same to?"

"Not for certain but I assumed the chap playing our vicar at one point, Craig something, must have said no to one of Josey's schemes because suddenly there were rumours and he was gone."

"There's nobody else you know?"

Gifford shook his head slowly. "I am sure there will be more but I don't know of anyone else."

"And there was nothing at the party that night that might be of use to us?"

Gifford shook his head again and Kate and Colm rose. As Colm collapsed the chairs and returned them to the building, Kate thanked Hugh Gifford.

"I am still angry with her, you know. Because she put a shade over my last few years with Rachel, but as I said before, I am too much of a coward to be your murderer."

Kate and Colm left Gifford sitting in his garden, face uplifted and eyes closed. Kate hoped he was remembering the better times with his wife.

CHAPTER 30

As they were walking back to the car, Kate's phone rang,

"Hi Alice, what have you got?"

"Hi boss. Just to let you know that we've found the Watters but they're in the wilds of Cumbria."

"Oh bugger! Someone is going to have to traipse up there."

Alice coughed, "I've taken the liberty of organising a video call. The Watters don't have a very good signal so they're going to a community hub. They'll ring through at seven this evening. Is that okay?" Alice sounded anxious.

"That's fine, Alice. If I'm not satisfied once I've spoken to them, I'll arrange to go and see them."

"Alice, will you ring Summer Loving and tell her we're on our way to her parents' house to continue our interview with her? Should be with her within the hour."

"Will do."

As Kate strapped in, Colm asked, "Could we do something about lunch on the way?" As if to emphasise the comment, Kate could plainly hear his stomach rumble.

"Sounds like a plan. Find somewhere en route."

Before they'd reached the end of the road Kate's phone rang again, "Yes Alice?"

"Summer Loving says she would prefer to talk to you at the station and will be here by three. Is that okay?"

"Yes. No problem. Colm and I are going to do a sandwich stop. Lunch on me, what do you want?"

Kate heard muttered discussion and then, "Ham and egg roll for Len and a cheese and salad for me boss."

"What about Sergeant Hughes?"

"He's been roped in for this Bagshaw case. Logging in the forensics stuff."

"Okay then, just the four of us."

"What do you make of that Colm?"

"Ms Loving thinks she is going to have to come clean and whatever it is she doesn't want her parents overhearing?"

Kate nodded thoughtfully. "Yes, I'd be tempted to read it that way."

"At her age I'm not sure I would have had any skeletons in my cupboard. And, to be honest, if it wasn't for fear of their reputations, both Masters' and Gifford's skeletons weren't earth shattering, were they?"

"No, but it's a revelation by our victim, and the way she did it. Letting the rumours start. It cost Masters his job and his place in Eashire."

"True."

"It's all about reputations isn't it? It's what

these people have in common. The need to keep their reputations. Someone said that a reputation is like a candle flame – easy to flicker and be blown out."

"Well, wouldn't that concern everyone? We all want to have good reputations, don't we?"

"Exactly! But when you're in the public eye, like in theatre, reputation is everything because it's all about image. And that's where our victim's power lay. She knew her audience's weakness and manipulated it to her own ends."

CHAPTER 31

Back at the station, once she had dropped off the letters Delver had found, Kate called Len and Alice to the meetings table and Colm gave out the sandwiches and cans. Whilst everyone ate, Kate began a summation of what they had so far.

"Feel free to add anything as I go," she began. "Okay, our victim was a blackmailer. She would befriend people, find out something unsavoury and threaten to go public if they didn't give her gifts or money or both. We have this now confirmed by Craig Masters, who refused to be blackmailed and lost his job and Hugh Gifford, who was paying irregular amounts."

Through a mouthful of cheese, Alice added, "And we have two monthly payments on her accounts that go back years."

"Yes. Where have we got with that?"

Alice wiped her mouth. "Forensics are snowed under but Zara Bakir said she'd try and get to it on Sunday."

"Right. We also have some interesting letters that were found with the victim's will by her solicitor this morning. In brief, they detail elements from our victim's past that she would not have wanted to be made public and a plea for her to mend her ways. Which I think was ignored, given the tone of the last letter."

"But," said Colm, "There is no explicit death threat in them. The last one you could argue has an implied threat."

"Agreed. I've made copies and left the originals with forensics. Like our tracking of the money, we're going to have to wait until after the weekend."

Colm wiped his mouth as he popped in the last of the sandwich. "We're pretty sure that the PA is not being totally honest with us. The solicitor said he heard Summer Loving's room door slam early in the night whereas the PA says she heard something at two fifteen. But she's not telling us everything, is she boss?"

"No, I don't think she is. And neither was Summer Loving, which is why we want to interview her again today."

"Interesting that she wants to come to the station again. Most people don't want to set foot in the place. Coppers included!" Len laughed.

Kate nodded her agreement. "Yes, whatever she's worried about coming out, she doesn't want her family to know."

"So do you think the Watters are involved?" Alice asked.

"They've got to be interviewed since they were amongst the last to leave the party. If not the last. We haven't yet confirmed what time they left or what time Salisbury and Purcell left. We have to tie up the time line."

"But you think the door slamming from

Summer Loving means she argued with someone, probably our victim?" Alice asked.

Kate nodded. "Yes. Although at the moment her statement says that she came to bed before everyone else had gone and didn't get a chance to talk with Grace about anything."

"But why would she lie?" Len asked, scratching his nose, "she knows we're going to find out it's a lie once we've spoken with everyone."

"Perhaps she thought we wouldn't track down the Watters. Especially, if they were the last to leave and would know Loving was still there," Alice surmised.

"Well, hopefully, we'll find out the truth of that a bit later today," said Kate looking at her watch. "Okay anything else anyone wants to add?"

No-one had, and so Colm and Kate looked over the notes from their previous discussion with Loving and what information they had gained that morning. As they lined up their questions, Kate wondered, not for the first time, why people persisted in lying to the police. With modern technology there were very few things they couldn't find out, eventually. It was the wasting time that Kate resented.

CHAPTER 32

At a few minutes to three Kate's desk phone rang and the front desk officer reported that Summer Loving was, once again, in the building. Not prepared to play nicely Kate asked for their visitor to be placed in one of the less salubrious interview rooms. She hoped that bolted down chairs and table and the anonymously grey walls would have a psychological impact on the actress.

She didn't look as blooming as she had on her first trip to see them. Kate could see the wariness in her eyes. She knew that Kate was tracking down her lies. "Thank you for coming back in to see us," she began. "We were quite happy to come out to you."

Loving gave a breathy laugh, "No, it's fine. I don't want my parents involved in all this. They have enough on their plates."

"We have been speaking with others who were at the party and they seem convinced that you were the last one to see Ms Grace. In fact that you had a bit of an argument with her." Kate waited.

Loving clasped and unclasped her hands and then looked intently at them before letting out a deep sigh. "I'm sorry I lied to you." She looked up and Kate held her stare.

Loving looked as though she didn't know where to start. Kate decided to load the die a little. "If I were to tell you that we have been told that some people felt befriended by Ms Grace and then she somehow betrayed that trust, would that help with your explanation?"

Loving breathed out deeply. "I didn't want to speak ill of the dead and I hadn't realised others had experienced a similar situation."

Kate nodded and hoped the silence would encourage further explanation. It did. "Please, can the following be kept out of the public eye?"

Kate was honest, "I can't guarantee that if your information proves vital to our case. However, if it merely confirms what we already know about Ms Grace then I cannot see it being of interest beyond this interview." Kate hoped that would suffice.

Still, Loving paused and then she squared her shoulders and looked directly at Kate. "In my line of work image and reputation are so important, especially when you are starting out." Kate nodded her understanding.

"So my agent has planned that my image is 'girl next door', a little 'unworldly'. So rumours about me having an abortion at eighteen would not sit well."

Kate waited for Loving to expand and hoped that her face was signalling the sympathy she felt.

"I'd finished with my boyfriend at the end

of school. I knew the relationship would not survive the separation of holiday time only and to be honest he was a sweet guy but I wanted to start my course as a free agent." Again, a pause. "Does that sound heartless?"

Kate shook her head, "It sounds quite realistic to me."

"Anyway, at the time when Josey was being very helpful, I found out I was pregnant. I didn't know what to do. I couldn't tell my parents and I wasn't going to tell Daniel, my ex, so I ended up telling Josey. She was amazing. Sympathetic but practical. I didn't want a child, not at eighteen with my whole life and potential career ahead of me, so Josey organised an abortion for me." She blew out a breath and sat back. Her eyes had moved to the floor but Kate was sure that they weren't seeing the grey linoleum tiles.

"She paid for everything and made a joke about paying her back when I was rich and famous. I never dreamt that she meant it or that the price would not be solely in monetary terms."

"Was she blackmailing you?" Colm was brutally frank.

Loving winced before looking back at Kate, "At first it was," she searched for the right words, "gentle nudging. 'Could I suggest to the director I was working for that she would be good for such and such a role.' I told her I couldn't do that. I was just starting out and although I'd got some good reviews I was in no position to bargain with directors. Then her nudging was underlined with 'it would be such a shame if your abortion became common knowledge'. She knew she had me over a barrel."

"But Ms Grace didn't appear in any productions with you, did she?"

Loving shook her head and chewed her bottom lip. "The night of the party. When she went missing. I tried to talk to her and explain how difficult it was for me to approach the director or the producers." Loving glanced at Kate, who gently nodded for her to continue.

"At first, she seemed to understand what I was trying to say but then she started to explain how she would approach them and that's what I should do. I tried to explain that it didn't work like that these days. Although I'm not sure that they ever worked the way she said. I got upset and began to raise my voice. And the more upset I became, the calmer and icier she became. In the end she sent me to bed!" Another glance at Kate.

"I was so angry. I flew up the stairs and slammed the door of my room. I'd forgotten about poor Mr Delver in the room next door."

"And that was the last time you saw Ms Grace?" Kate prodded.

"Honestly, yes. I think it was only the fact that I had been on the go since six that morning that meant I slept. I didn't know what to do. Josey could ruin me."

"That would seem like a good motive to kill her, to me," said Colm quietly.

Loving's head shot up and she glared at him. "I know, which is why I lied to you when I first came in. I knew you wouldn't believe me. I was the last one to see her and I had a blazing row with her. Perfect motive and opportunity. But please believe me. I didn't kill her. I left her in the front lounge with a glass of wine in her hands, smiling patronisingly at me."

"Did you notice anyone else hanging around the house or garden?"

Loving shook her head. "I wasn't really looking. I assumed everyone had gone. I knew Claire had gone up earlier, as had Mr Delver."

"Were the doors to the garden still open when you went to bed?"

Loving looked thoughtful, "I didn't notice." A pause. "When we moved through from the conservatory to the lounge they were still open, so unless Claire closed them before going up I assume they were left open." Another pause. "Thinking about it, the lights were still on in the garden. I remember I went to close the curtains and thought how magical it all looked."

"Were they still on the following morning?"

"I didn't notice. It was another bright, sunny morning and I think their twinkle would have been lost in the sunlight."

"And when you got up you didn't notice anything out of place? Different? Unexpected?"

A shake of the head. "No, nothing. Claire was in the kitchen so I stuck my head round and said I was off and left."

Kate looked across to Colm for any further questions but he shook his head. "Thank you for your honesty Ms Loving."

"My story isn't likely to be leaked, is it?"

"Not from us. Ms Loving."

Kate and Colm left. Outside the room Kate asked Colm to sort out the paperwork, "And then get yourself off. Bright and early at the station tomorrow."

"Will do. Thanks boss."

CHAPTER 33

Returning to the office, Kate sent Len and Alice home. "The work will still be here on Monday but perhaps by then forensics will have something to help us focus down on things." Kate sat down at her desk and flicked through the messages that had been placed there. "Thanks for arranging the train and tickets, Len."

"No problem. Thanks, boss."

Kate looked at another note. "Alice, can you run through this video call for me?"

Alice walked across and nodded at the slip of paper in Kate's hand. "You need to set up a meeting. Then you'll get an access code that you'll need to text to the Watters." Seeing the look of panic that slid across Kate's face, she smiled, "And I've arranged for Zara to come up and set it up for you."

"You did that deliberately, didn't you?"

Alice laughed. "She also said she would stay here while you were online, in case of technical glitches. You won't mind if she eats while you're talking do you?"

"If she is helping me out with technology she can bring a three course meal in!"

Alice laughed. "Enjoy London and see you on Monday."

"Thanks, Alice."

In the quiet of the office Kate spread out the copies of the letters Delver had found. Something she had seen or heard today was niggling at the back of her mind. She hoped if she went back over everything it would surface.

She looked again at the letters as an object. They looked to have all been torn out of the same type of notepad, if not the same one. As far as she could see, it was the type you could buy anywhere.

Kate then looked at the writing. It was a careful hand. Letters were well formed and regular; almost featureless. The contents seemed educated, perhaps a little stilted. Each letter was in two halves; that dealing with their victims present activities and then her supposed past. If their investigations were anything to go by, the writer was correct about her recent misdemeanours. So could they suppose that it was also right about her past? Who was their letter writer? Generally, malicious letters were written by women. Although, could you call the contents malicious? In the main they accurately depicted the life and times of Josephine Grace. She couldn't see a woman, on her own, being able to move a dead body.

Kate stopped. What proof did they have that Grace had been killed at the house? Kate leant back in her chair and rested her head on the back of it. She gazed sightlessly at the ceiling. She'd been assuming that Grace had been dead before she left the house but what if she'd been lured to somewhere else, even the burial site? Kate let the idea mull and then sat up and shook her head. She didn't think it was likely. How would she have got there? Didn't the PA say that she would have heard any car pulling up onto the drive?

That brought her to another conundrum; what had the PA heard, or even seen, that night? Kate's gut told her that there was something Claire Bayntry was not telling them. She made herself a note on her to do list. They needed to talk to Bayntry again and prise it out of her.

Kate was almost tempted to send Alice or Len to bring her back to the station. Maybe the shock of that would loosen her tongue. She'd think about that.

Now to Colm's reports about the interviews he and Alice had conducted at REAl Radio. Half an hour later Kate made another note: Tamara Cullen needed to be talked to again. She sighed heavily. Why did people insist on editing the truth? Was it about reputation again?

Kate pulled her hands through her hair. A sure sign that she was feeling frustrated. Were the letters important? Who was the author? Her gut was telling her they were and that it was a man. She couldn't see a woman carrying a dead body or digging the grave and what about the fungus? That was specialist knowledge about its rapid decomposition properties, even if anyone could grow a mushroom.

CHAPTER 34

Kate's reverie was interrupted by a knock at the open door and PC Zara Bakir poked her head round. "Alice said you might need help with setting up your online meeting?"

"No *might* about it! Come in and work your magic."

Kate marvelled that despite the lateness of the day and that she'd been on duty all day, Zara still looked fresh and composed. Her only concession was she'd removed her cravat. Kate vacated her seat and Zara took over the controls of her computer.

Although watching, Kate wasn't really seeing. Mentally, she was going over what she wanted to ask the Watters. Would they provide the breakthrough? Surely something had to give on this case, and soon. She was brought back to the room by Zara's question, "Shall I text the address to your witnesses, ma'am?"

"Yes, please and no *ma'am*. Either Kate or boss is absolutely fine."

Zara smiled, "Yes, boss." She then texted through the details to the Watters. "Shall I talk you through?"

"Please."

"Okay, you are hosting this meeting, so when your interviewees type in the address I've just sent, you will see them appear on your screen. Make sure this icon," she pointed to a microphone symbol, "is on, otherwise they won't hear you. Other than that you don't need to touch anything else, just ask your questions. Okay?"

Kate nodded and hoped it was as simple as Zara made out. "I'll just sit out of sight, over there," Zara pointed to Alice's desk, "and have my tea and be on hand, just in case."

At that moment the computer made a noise and two faces appeared on her screen. Zara vacated the chair and Kate sat. "Good evening Mr and Mrs Watters. Thank you for agreeing to this meeting."

The two heads nodded and Andy Watters said, "Whatever we can do to help. We always thought Josey had been murdered but still it's a shock when you're proved right." His wife, Christine Barford, as was, nodded her head in agreement.

"Did you know Ms Grace well?"

This time Christine decided to answer, "Not really. We were only in the cast for a few months."

"And yet you stayed until the very end, I understand."

The couple looked at one another before Andy Watters answered. He cleared his throat and both looked a little uncomfortable. "Christine and I weren't married at that point.

Well, not to one another, anyway."

Christine took over the explanation. "Being at Josey's party meant we could be together without arousing suspicion from our former spouses."

"Didn't they come, too? Or expect to come?"

Again the pair looked abashed, "We told them it was cast members only," Andy explained.

"So, who remained until the end of the party?"

They both looked thoughtful and then Christine said, "Two of Josey's London friends, Gerald Purcell and Richard Salisbury. They were a bit unsettled because they'd ordered a taxi and it was late picking them up. Once they'd gone it was just us and Summer Loving."

"I got the impression that Summer wanted us gone, didn't you?" Andy addressed his wife.

Slowly, she nodded her head, "Yes, you could be right. The atmosphere certainly became a little uncomfortable and we left about ten minutes after the London pair."

"What time was that?"

They both screwed up their faces in thought, "Gerald said they'd ordered the taxi for midnight and it was late. He rang the firm again and the controller said it was ten minutes away."

"Yes, but he didn't ring until the taxi was already ten minutes late so they must have left about twenty minutes after midnight." Andy was making the calculations.

"And we only stayed another ten, maybe fifteen minutes. So it must have been just after twelve-thirty when we left," agreed Christine.

"Did you drive or order a taxi? And did you go straight home?"

Andy shook his head. "I drove and we found a quiet lane and sat and chatted for another hour or so. I didn't drop Chrissie off until almost two."

Again Christine Watters nodded, "My ex-husband commented at how late I was back and had it been a good party. I apologised for losing track of time." She blushed afresh at her deceit.

Andy tried to justify their actions, "We're not proud of the way we behaved back then. We were both smitten and knew we wanted to spend the rest of our lives together. We divorced as soon as we could."

Christine merely blushed a deeper hue of pink and avoided eye contact.

For the time being Kate could think of nothing else she wished to ask. She thought these two were on the level. If she found out anything more about them she would be back for more. "Thank you both for your time. You have been very helpful in allowing us to confirm the time line on that evening."

"Glad we could help," Andy replied.

Kate was now at the point where she didn't know what the etiquette was for ending the call. Fortunately, the Watters signed off and Zara appeared over the screen and pointed to a button for Kate to click on. She did and her screen returned to saver mode.

Having thanked Zara for her help and for being on stand-by, Kate decided it was time to go home. She would stop off for a takeaway. She hadn't got the energy to cook, not even a ping meal.

CHAPTER 35

Sitting in her lounge gazing sightlessly at the telly, Kate savoured her scrumptious fish and chips covered in a generous helping of salt in vinegar. She'd bought a sausage for Monster and after she'd cut it up and allowed it to cool, he had devoured it and was now sitting by the armchair appreciatively washing himself. Kate took a sip from her can of dandelion and burdock. She'd seen the can in the chip shop and suddenly had a burst of nostalgia... Her mum and her sitting on the hearth of their new home waiting for Dad and his friends to turn up with the furniture van. She couldn't have been more than four. They'd sat eating sausage and chips and drinking dandelion and burdock. Even now, she could recall the echoey sound of their voices in the empty room and the taste of the drink between the greasiness of the chips. Kate smiled to herself, happy days.

Kate replayed the day's events and then groaned. "Damn!" She'd left the profiles on Purcell and Salisbury on her desk. She'd meant to pick them up and study them on the train. Colm would need to pass the office on his way to the railway station, would he pick them up for her? She texted. A few minutes later he replied, "No problemo."

The niggle still hadn't made itself known and Kate tried to concentrate on the television programme. Give her brain a rest from the case. But instead of being fascinated by the science of DNA, she found her mind wandering to the proposed night out with Jude and her friends tomorrow. Part of her was wishing she'd never said yes. She wouldn't know anyone apart from Jude and what if Jude was with someone? She'd certainly be a gooseberry.

Another part of her, which interestingly always took on the voice of her best friend Siobhan, told her to pull herself together. She and Siobhan had become friends in Year 10. Prior to that they'd been aware of one another in the school but in Year 10 they'd been thrown together by both their choice of GCSEs and their ability. Siobhan had been the first one Kate had shared her feelings with and her response had been, "Oh that's good. I don't have to compete with you for the boys!" She'd laughed and hugged Kate tightly and added, "I think I knew and I'm just a little miffed that you don't fancy me!"

They'd gone to the same university and shared digs. Kate had seen Siobhan through a devastating break up of her first true love and then Siobhan had reciprocated. Kate had been Siobhan's only bridesmaid and it was to her that Kate had turned when her relationship with Robyn hit the rocks. They had the kind of friendship that meant even though they lived miles away from one another, whenever they met up it was just like picking up again from where they'd left off.

Now, Siobhan was telling her to go and sort out what she wanted to wear for tomorrow night. Kate got to her feet and did as she was told. In her bedroom she opened her wardrobe wide and stared. Were jeans too casual? She had a black pair that she'd worn only once. Mind you, she'd only worn them once because they had been a bit tight. Now she tried them on and was delighted that her sessions at the gym meant they fitted snugly but not tightly. Right, jeans. Now a nice shirt. She had lots of white and plain shirts. They were her daily work uniform. What about a bit of colour? There was a gorgeous sage green silk shirt. She heard Siobhan's voice, "That looks lovely with your colour hair." Kate tried on the shirt with the jeans. Yes. She thought she looked okay. As she was staring at her image, she felt she was being watched. She spun round seeking out the spy. Nothing and then she saw Monster. He clearly had followed her up the stairs and was sat in the doorway watching her every move. Kate laughed and asked him, "What do you think, Monster?" He observed her for a few minutes and then turned and walked away.

Kate checked her watch. Nearly ten-thirty. Time for Monster to go out and for her to get ready for bed. It would be an early start tomorrow.

LIN BIRD

CHAPTER 36

Kate stood in the cool shade of the platform. It was eight o'clock and the clear blue sky promised another hot day. Kate stood waiting for Colm to join her. The platform was surprisingly quiet, unless, everyone had decided moving towards the coast was a better bet than going in land. Kate also wished she was not heading for London. It was always hotter and more humid in town. The streets seemed to hold the heat and stop any breeze. Not that there was much of a wind, even here.

Colm appeared, carrying a rucksack. He'd adopted a pale jacket and trousers but still appeared smart and business like. Kate hoped they wouldn't get too grimy in the city, especially when they used the underground. It always seemed to have smut in the air. He waved his hand in acknowledgement and Kate joined him at the gate to show the train employee their printed tickets.

"Thanks for dropping into the office. It saved me a journey."

"Not a problem. I was going in early anyway to type up yesterday's interviews. I thought you might like to review them on our journey."

"Oh great. Thanks Colm."

Further conversation was prevented by the

tannoy announcing the arrival of their train. As it slowed before them Kate looked for carriage B. Len had reserved them a couple of seats with a table, in case they wanted to work. Carriage B went past and Kate began to follow it. Few passengers got off and it seemed that Kate and Colm were the only ones getting on.

They found their seats, with a table, as promised. Apart from a young woman at the other end of the carriage, with earbuds in, they were the only passengers. Having settled, Colm reached into his rucksack and removed several folders before placing it in the luggage rack.

Their seats were side by side and Kate suggested that they go through the profiles of Purcell and Salisbury simultaneously. Each using a highlighter, provided by Colm, they marked off the times when the two actors had worked with their victim. Twenty minutes or so later, Kate leant back in her seat and stretched her neck from its crick. "Okay, our two men have known each other, on and off, for the last thirty years."

Colm agreed, "But didn't really come across Grace until they were all in that period drama, Faringers, that started in 2000, so they'd known her fifteen years or so at the time of her death."

"Not sure I watched that series."

"I remember it, nine o'clock on a Sunday evening. The music always made me feel sad because it signalled the end of the weekend,"

Colm mused.

"They don't seem to have worked together since. Well, Purcell and Salisbury do, but not Grace."

"In fact it looks like the series was a launch for those two in terms of television roles. They both go on to take parts in all the popular series of the 2000s. Not that they were ever in the same episodes."

"So, the period drama is a launch for the two men but it's not long after it that Grace is talking about retirement."

"She was head-hunted by REAl Radio and it's kept her name in the public."

Kate stared out of the window, musing on the information they had. That was part of the problem. They had so much general information but nothing she could hone in on for the murder. She voiced her thoughts, "Fifteen years is plenty of time for Grace to find dirt on them so do you think their relationship was a genuine friendship or one of power play?"

"Well, given her form, I'm inclined to think that she probably had something on each of them. Some indiscretion when they were starting out."

"Yes, but something which would damage their reputation now."

Colm agreed. He stood and stretched. He had barely managed to fit his long legs under the table. "Do you want coffee?"

"I would love coffee but I don't think there's a buffet car."

Colm smiled and reached for his rucksack. In a few minutes he was pouring coffee from a flask. Kate sniffed appreciatively, "Is this real coffee, you know, ground beans and such?"

Colm's smile burst into a grin, "I stopped at our favourite coffee shop and asked if they'd fill my flask. Afraid it had to be flat white but I did bring sugar."

"I like your initiative, Constable."

Settled back in their seats with the coffee, Kate half turned to Colm, "Seriously, I've been meaning to have a career chat with you. Isn't it time you took your sergeant's exams? You'd get my support."

Colm blushed a little, "Do you think I'm ready, seriously?"

"Absolutely. I was thinking about saying to Alice that she should think about moving across to CID as well. Then I was going to suggest to Bart that our little team of five ought to be permanent."

"Len as well?"

Kate laughed, "Yes, Len as well. He does work for us, doesn't he?"

Colm had to agree. Known for his work-shy approach throughout the station, Len seemed to have taken a shine to Kate and was actually helpful. "Do you think Bart would go for it?"

"Well, our clear up rate has been good. If

we can get this case cracked, we might have a winning hand." Kate looked thoughtful before asking, "Did anything strike you as important yesterday in our interviews?"

Colm paused and reflected before answering, "Well, we think Bayntry is still hiding something and Gifford and Loving have confirmed our view of Grace as a blackmailer." He paused again. "What we haven't got is a viable suspect. Did the Watters prove useful?"

Kate shook her head. "No, not really. Basically they were having an affair and stayed on at the party just to have time together. I'll get Len or Alice to check their alibi on Monday but my gut feeling is they aren't our suspects. Doesn't mean we won't double check but I can't see them having a motive."

"What if Grace threatened to reveal their affair?"

"No. They were already planning their divorces and getaway. I don't think revelation would have caused them any additional problems."

"So, what do you think we had yesterday?"

Kate shook her head and sighed in exasperation, "I wish I knew. I just think that there was something I should have picked up on. Let me read your reports."

CHAPTER 37

Kate read and re-read Colm's reports. Nothing jumped out. Frustrated, she packed the pages away and looked out of the window. She'd always enjoyed train journeys. The anonymity it allowed as you peered at people's homes or drivers waiting at level crossings. Even the passengers waiting on the platform. She reflected on the beauty of the British countryside. Not a lover of heat, she often holidayed in her home country and thought too many people ignored the stunning natural scenery of the United Kingdom, its islands and dependencies. Thinking that sunshine and beaches were the only model for a wonderful holiday.

Colm interrupted her thoughts. "Nothing jumping out?"

"No," running fingers through her hair, "I know there was something. I just hope it comes to me soon."

"Let it lie. Think about something else. It normally works for me."

Kate agreed. "You're right." She sought to engage in some social chat. "Sorry I had to drag you off to London today. I hope it didn't ruin your plans." Kate was fishing. She hadn't forgotten Colm's response when she'd told him about this trip nor the surreptitious phone call shortly after.

Colm went a very pretty shade of pink and Kate was glad that their carriage was still fairly empty with no-one witnessing his discomfort. Kate hastened to put him out of his misery, "Sorry. It's none of my business."

Colm rubbed his chin. "No, you're fine. I'd arranged to go out for the day with a girl, Jenna. I met her through the Young Farmers group."

"Good for you. I was worried you were turning into a confirmed bachelor," Kate joshed him.

"No. It's about someone not getting upset about strange shifts and the demands of the work. Or changing plans." He raised a quizzical eyebrow at her. "You must have the same problem?"

"True." She almost added that it was the cause of her last break up but really that wasn't true. It was partly about that but also about Robyn's infidelity. "So what's she like? Or would you prefer not to discuss Jenna?" Secretly hoping that he did.

Colm smiled. "She's a nurse and five years younger than me. Her parents have a small holding and she is friends with one of my sisters. She has a good sense of humour and likes a laugh. We've had a couple of sort of dates," seeing Kate's puzzled expression, "we met up with a group thing so we were there together but it didn't need to be."

Kate thought she understood. "So, even more reason to go for your sergeant's."

Colm held up his hands. "We're only going out. You sound like you've got me married and settled down, needing more income."

Kate laughed, "Sorry, but it is time for your sergeant's. Mind you, will you have time, if Jenna is around?"

"I'm sure I will. She still wants to go out and about with the group of friends she's created, so we won't be bound at the hips."

"So, what was today's trip going to be?"

Colm grinned. "I was going to pack up a picnic and take her to Samford Woods. There are some lovely walks there and several places we could stop to rest and eat."

"It's not somewhere I've been," Kate admitted. In all honesty she knew very little of the area around Eashire, unless a case took her there.

"Anyway, we've rescheduled for tomorrow. In fact it might be better tomorrow because there's due to be a bit of a breeze and a little cloud cover. Perfect walking weather."

"Well, I wish you well. Both for the trip tomorrow and with Jenna, if she turns out to be the one for you."

Colm grinned, "There you go again. She's just someone I've met."

Kate smiled her apology and then began to

gather up their files. She could see along the length of the train that they were coming into Paddington.

CHAPTER 38

Kate had already planned their route from Paddington to the actors' homes. Both lived within walking distance of the West End. Purcell in Newgate Street and about a ten minute walk to Salisbury's place in Bedford Row. The easiest route was to use the underground. Kate knew they needed the Central line. She set off at a brisk pace with Colm close behind.

Although Colm was not a country bumpkin, Kate could see that he was out of his comfort zone. For Kate it was like coming back to a pool you once knew well. Familiar but not homely. Fortunately, with it being Saturday, there was not the usual cramming on the tube. Busy but not manic. More relaxed somehow. Kate had hated the days when she'd had to travel by tube in the height of the rush hour.

Once on the tube, Kate checked her own notebook for the address of Gerald Purcell. According to the maps, it was a short walk from Holborn station to Newgate Street. As Kate had feared, the streets of London retained the heat of the last few weeks' torridity. Slipping her jacket off, she folded it over one arm.

"Do you want to put it in my rucksack?" Colm asked.

"No, thanks. I'll put it back on when we go in

to interview. Even if we then ask if they mind if we take jackets off. Need to appear business like."

Colm stopped before an antique shop. He peered through the window and then looked at the door. "It makes you know you can't afford anything if you need to make an appointment," he said. Nodding at the polite notice on the door.

"Right. This is the address, so I'm assuming Purcell must have the flat above." Kate looked up. There were two storeys above the shop. "So where's the entrance?"

The door was a discreet black one to one side of the shop. The only indication that it led somewhere was the presence of the knocker. Nothing else indicated its use. Colm rapped loudly and responded to Kate's grimace, "If it's got to be heard up there it needs to be firm."

They waited several minutes. Kate was irritated. Purcell knew they were coming this morning and they had arrived at the appointed time. She was about to give her own rap when the door opened and a smartly dressed man opened it. Kate knew that Gerald Purcell was in his mid-forties but he could have passed for younger. Hair that once had been blond had now darkened and was a contrast to the white blond of his eyebrows and the Cavalier style moustache and beard he sported. He had the face of a Cavalier, Kate decided and certainly the voice.

"DI Medlar? Sorry to have kept you. I was on the phone to my agent. Please come in." He left the door open, turned and began to mount a broad wooden staircase with an old fashioned stair runner and carpet stays, she hadn't seen since her grandma's house. The air was pleasantly cool and smelt of something citrus.

Purcell led them into a tall ceilinged room with two large windows that respected both light and air. Kate wondered if the flat had been furnished by the antique dealer below.

Purcell indicated a set of chairs and hovered over them as they sat. "Can I get you some refreshments? Homemade lemonade? This weather is so dehydrating."

Kate thanked him and agreed to his offer. She and Colm sat in silence as Purcell disappeared to bring the drinks. Kate knew that Purcell owned a cottage in Wales and wondered whether he owned or rented this flat. She'd put Alice onto that. The furniture was mainly wooden and well looked after but curiously the flat was devoid of personal items. No photographs, ornaments, not even a book laid aside.

Purcell returned and set a silver tray on the coffee table in front of Kate and Colm. The lemonade was in large Champagne flutes. Purcell took one for himself and sat opposite them. "Now, I know you've solved the mystery of Josey's disappearance, so how can I help?"

"Unfortunately, solving that mystery has led to another: who murdered her?"

Purcell spluttered into his glass, "Murder?!

David, my agent, didn't explain." With an unsteady hand he put his glass onto a table at his elbow. "I had no idea."

Kate thought he seemed genuinely upset but she reminded herself that he was a well-respected actor. "I'm sorry to have sprung that information on you but we do need to ask some questions about your relationship with Ms Grace."

Purcell removed a handkerchief from his trouser pocket, as yet unused, and now used it to mop his brow and lips. "Of course. My goodness, murder!"

Colm sat patiently with his open notebook and Kate took a breath to begin when Purcell put up a hand to stop her. "Please, would you excuse me? I need to... er." Without finishing his sentence or waiting for a reply he got up and left the room.

CHAPTER 39

"Well, that seems to have knocked him off balance," Colm observed.

"Emm. Strangely so?"

"Not sure. I suppose if they were good friends it would hit him hard. I wonder why the agent hadn't made it clear why we were interviewing him?"

"Perhaps he thought it was obvious; we'd found Grace's body, so an enquiry is underway. Don't know."

At this point Purcell returned. "My apologies. In retrospect I should have realised this was a murder enquiry. You don't expect that sort of thing to happen to people you know, do you?"

Kate nodded her understanding. "Are you up to answering a few questions for us, sir?"

"Yes. Yes. Go ahead."

"I understand you first met Josephine Grace when you were in the Faringer series?"

Thoughtful, Purcell looked up. "Actually, we had worked together before that. It was a small, not particularly successful play in the late 1990s. Josey was the star and I was third attendant, or something similar." He gave a self-deprecating laugh. "But really, Faringer was the main connection."

"How long did you work together?"

"Faringer ran for six series but Josey was only in the first two. Me, and Dickie Salisbury were in one, two and most of three."

"So you must have spent a lot of time with her on set?" Kate continued.

Again, Purcell was thoughtful. "It varied really. Did you watch the series?" He glanced between the two detectives. Both shook their heads. "The basic premise was that the eponymous Faringer was an industrialist in the latter third of the Victorian era. Josey played his wife. I played their son and Dickie played the son of their arch enemy. So I had quite a few scenes with Josey at the start of the first series but then she and Faringer were faded out and Dickie and I were centre stage. But by the middle of series three our offspring were becoming the leading figures."

"So, would you say all three of you were friends?"

Purcell nodded vigorously. "Oh yes. In fact Dickie and his wife, Cheryl, became firm friends with Josey and if they went out together they often invited me to make up a foursome."

"Were you surprised when Ms Grace moved to Eashire?"

Purcell looked thoughtful once more and began to answer hesitantly, "Josey had stopped getting major roles and said she wasn't prepared to be a 'has been in some third rate television soap'. Or words to that effect."

"So the offer from REAl Radio was a saving grace for her?"

"Yes, I suppose so."

"Would you talk us through the day of the party? Your actions. Anything you noticed."

Purcell leant his head against the chair back and closed his eyes. After several minutes he began, "I wasn't working in the theatre at the time so decided to take Josey up on her invite."

"Did Ms Grace often invite you to her home in Eashire?"

"No, not often but she would like us there to remind others of her past glories!" He smiled at the thought.

"So, the party with all the team for Peaceford was a perfect opportunity to show off."

Purcell's smile grew, "Exactly. Dickie was also going down so we'd arranged to take the lunchtime train because the later ones would be packed with Friday commuters."

"What time did you arrive in Eashire?"

"We were due in at three-seventeen but there'd been a bit of a delay at..," he paused and seemed to be scouring his memories, "so we pulled into Eashire at three-thirty-six. Not too much of a delay."

"You have an excellent memory to recall such detail after all this time, sir," Colm interrupted.

Purcell waved his hand. "No, not really. We were quizzed about all these details when Grace went missing so they are imprinted on my brain."

"Did you go straight to your hotel from the station?"

"We did. We stayed at The Grand. I wanted a bath and a nap so I arranged to meet Dickie in the restaurant at six for a light supper before heading to Josey's."

"How did you get to Ms Grace's house?"

"The hotel organised a taxi and we got there for just after seven-forty. Dickie arranged with the chap to come back for us at midnight but he didn't turn up."

"How was the party? Did you notice any animosity? Disputes?"

"No!" Purcell laughed. "Josey and all her sycophants were in the conservatory. It was a lovely evening, weather wise, and people were strolling around the gardens."

Kate pushed, "So nobody seemed unhappy or out of place?"

Another pause.

"Well, I did notice her solicitor, Gordon Delver, seemed a little down at the mouth and Josey was deliberately ignoring his sulk."

Kate's ears pricked and she sought clarification, "Gordon Delver seemed unhappy? With Josey or just generally unhappy?"

"I'd say with Josey but I couldn't swear to it."

"You say there was a problem with the return taxi. What time did you leave the party in the end?"

"I don't know exactly, but I'd say, about twenty-past midnight, perhaps five minutes later."

"And you went straight back to the hotel?"

"We did. The porter saw us in. I'm sure he'll remember us," he grinned, which was quite disarming and took years off his countenance, "Dickie gave him Juliet's balcony speech and explained that 'Where fore art thou?' did not mean where was Romeo but why was he a Montague. He got quite heated about it."

"Did you go straight back to London the following morning?"

Was it Kate's imagination or did he look a little uncomfortable?

"No, we were due to meet up with Josey again Saturday evening. Just for old time's sake!"

"So, when did you find out that Ms Grace had gone missing?"

"When Claire telephoned the hotel. That must have been early afternoon. She was distraught. Didn't think the police were taking it seriously. We offered to go round but she said she had Gordon there so we decided to catch the five ten back to London."

"Was it you, Ms Bayntry spoke to?"

"Err... no. Claire spoke with Dickie and he relayed the information."

"Can you think of anyone who had a grudge against Ms Grace? Who would wish her harm?"

"Josey! No of course not."

Again, Kate's instinct detected something in Purcell's body language. What was he hiding? He definitely wasn't telling them the whole truth. She pushed again. "You had known Ms Grace for almost fifteen years and in that time nobody fell out with her?"

Purcell's discomfort increased. "I'm sure she must have fallen out with people but I am not aware of anyone."

"You couldn't even hazard a guess?"

Purcell shook his head. His colour was becoming warmer. Kate tried to think of another way of repeating the question and pushing him just that little more. "There have been no rumours? I imagine the acting world is quite a small pond and everyone knows everyone else."

His retort was a little sharp. "One may know of other people but it doesn't mean that one knows, or listens, to gossip."

Kate conceded defeat. She'd try that one again if she ever had more information. Checking with Colm, through a head tilt, that he had no further questions, Kate stood and held out her hand. "Thank you for your time, Mr Purcell. And I'm sorry the murder element was not made clearer to you."

Purcell rose too and shook hands with them both before leading then back to the front door.

CHAPTER 40

"What was your impression?" Kate asked as they walked away from Purcell's flat.

Colm stopped mid-stride and considered this question. "I don't understand why he didn't realise this was a murder enquiry and he seemed uncomfortable when you asked about people falling out with our victim." He continued to walk. "I maybe wrong but I don't get the impression he would act on his own. If he is part of the murder I think he was an accomplice."

"Richard Salisbury?"

"Well, they seem close, Dickie this and Dickie that. But how did they know about the preservation order on the trees and how did they get the body to the field?"

"I know the misper team looked to see if Grace had hired a car. I wonder if they thought to check other guests' names." She pulled out her own notebook and jotted down the task for later. "Richard Salisbury next. It's about a ten minute stretch. Come on."

Bedford Row was a step up from Purcell's flat over the antiques shop. Georgian fronted houses with tall paned sash windows towered over the street. On inspection at the bell push they discovered that the houses were divided into apartments. "Note that, Colm. These are apartments, not flats!" Kate said, tongue firmly in her cheek. There were no name plates alongside the bells for each apartment but Kate knew the Salisburys were on the middle floor. She pressed. Nothing was heard outside but suddenly a speaker crackled and a deep voice asked, "May I help you?"

Kate bent in, "DI Kate Medlar and DC Colm Hunter to see Richard Salisbury."

Simultaneously, the voice said, "Come up." And the door clicked open.

A large chandelier dominated the pale marble foyer. Kate made for the wide sweeping staircase that led to the first floor. On reaching that level, a door opened. Richard Salisbury was shorter in stature than Purcell but conveyed a sense of solidity and confidence. His dark hair was short and there were touches of grey at his temples. He was dressed casually in jeans and a red shirt. He walked towards them with his hand out in front of him and shook both their hands, "I'm sorry you had to come to London but we're both in work at the moment and you have to strike while the iron's hot."

Kate mouthed platitudes and followed Salisbury into a large room that benefitted from the tall windows they'd noted from outside. Tasteful furnishings but no antiques. The room glowed a soft green with darker splashes from the curtains and the suite. Sat on the sofa was a woman of about forty, Kate thought, who looked like she'd just stepped out of a celebrity magazine. Kate was sure that when she stood up she would be willowy!

Salisbury made the introductions, "My wife, Cheryl." She did not rise but held her hand out to be shaken. That task done, Kate and Colm took the two chairs and Salisbury joined his wife on the sofa. He settled back and for all intents and purposes looked calm and alert; it was the swivelling of his wedding ring that hinted that he was not as composed as he would have them think.

"Just to be clear," Kate started, "this is a murder enquiry. Mr Purcell seemed surprised by that fact."

"Oh poor Gerry. He can be very naïve," Salisbury said with just a hint of a smile.

"As long as you are clear?" Kate reiterated. Salisbury nodded his understanding.

"How long had you known Ms Grace when she went missing in 2015?"

Salisbury looked thoughtful before answering, "I think we first met her in early 2000. We were part of the drama, Faringer. So about fifteen years."

"And were you close?"

"Very, while we were all together in Faringer, probably less so since she retired to Eashire."

"And was that the same for Mr Purcell?"

"I'm sure he's told you that they worked together once before Faringer, but Josey was the star and he was third attendant, or something similar, so not really in her sphere."

"Would you say you always got on well with Ms Grace?"

Again that thoughtful pose, "I think we did. Would you say so, Cher?"

For the first time Cheryl Salisbury looked like she was in the room. "Yes. We did. Josey and I would natter about all sorts whilst the boys talked shop and stuff."

"The boys?" Kate wanted clarification.

"Dickie and Gerry. They've been friends for ever."

Kate thought it was time to move on. "Please would you talk through what happened the day of the party?"

Salisbury broke the eye contact he had made a point of maintaining when Kate spoke to him. Now, he looked over her shoulder. "Gerry was also going down so we'd arranged to take the lunchtime train because the later ones would be packed with Friday commuters."

"What time did you arrive in Eashire?"

"We were due in at three-seventeen but there'd been a bit of a delay at..," he paused, "so we pulled into Eashire at three-thirty-six. Not too much of a delay."

"What time were you expected at the party?"

"We thought we'd aim for about eight and leave at midnight. Give Josey her pound of flesh." Salisbury laughed but Kate wondered at his turn of phrase.

"What did you do between arrival at the station and arriving at Ms Grace's home?"

Again, that stare over her shoulder. "We stayed at The Grand. Gerry wanted a bath and a nap so I arranged to meet him in the restaurant at six for a light supper before heading to Josey's."

"And what did you do?"

"I used the minibar and went through a script I'd just been sent for about an hour and then had a quick shower and went to meet Gerry."

"How did you get to Ms Grace's house?"

"The hotel organised a taxi and we got there for about seven-forty. I arranged with the chap to come back for us at midnight but he didn't turn up." The frustration was evident in his tone.

"So, what time did you leave Ms Grace's home?"

Salisbury scratched his head, "I think the taxi was about twenty minutes late, after having put a rocket up the controller."

"And you went straight back to the hotel?"

He nodded and Kate continued, "When were you due back to London?"

"Not until Sunday, we were due to meet up with Josey again Saturday evening. Just for old time's sake!"

"So, when did you find out that Ms Grace had gone missing?"

"When Claire telephoned me at the hotel.

That must have been early afternoon. She was distraught. Didn't think the police were taking it seriously. We offered to go round but she said she had Gordon there so we decided to catch the five-ten back to London."

"Can you think of anyone who might have a grudge against Ms Grace?"

Another play of thoughtfulness, "I really can't."

"I understand you didn't go to the party, Mrs Salisbury?"

"Cheryl or Ms Harper, please. I didn't take Dickie's name when we married."

"My apologies Ms Harper. But you didn't go? Were you not invited?"

Ms Harper gave a little laugh, "I was invited but, unfortunately, the event clashed with a charity fundraiser I was hosting here in London."

"Cheryl is a charity fundraiser. Makes millions, don't you sweetheart?"

Ms Harper merely gave a small smile.

"What was the party like?"

"Err, like?"

"Was everyone happy? Did you notice anyone not happy or an argument?"

"No. It was a great night. I had a few words with Josey but she was busy with all her admirers; that's partly why we arranged to stay on and see her later on the Saturday."

Kate was sure he was lying. His wedding

ring must have been dizzy with the amount of turning it was enduring. Kate thought she'd go in for the kill, "Some people have suggested that Ms Grace had a tendency to use information against them. Did you ever experience anything like that?"

Salisbury was now rigid with his need to stay calm, "I'm amazed. Are you sure this isn't just someone with a grudge?"

Ms Harper also added her affirmation, "Josey was a wonderful person. I think that is a scandalous thing to say."

Kate was sure she wouldn't get anything more from Salisbury at the moment. Perhaps a visit to Eashire station might loosen his tongue. He and Purcell both.

CHAPTER 41

Back on the street, Kate raised an eyebrow in Colm's direction. "Did you find some of that a little..." she searched for the right word, "rehearsed?"

"Yep! And they were using the same script. Some of their phrases were identical. Do you think they'd arranged their story between them?"

"I think they did. And did you notice how uncomfortable they both became when I suggested some people might hold a grudge? They're holding something back."

"Do you think Grace was blackmailing them as well?"

"Why not?"

"That seems to be the basis for most, if not all, of her *friendships*," Kate emphasised the last word. "If we walk back to Paddington, if we see a restaurant or café that seems okay, we'll have some food. That sound okay?"

"Great by me. Breakfast seems a long time ago."

Not many minutes later they were being seated in an American style diner. Complete with Formica tables, banquettes and a 1950s juke box. Having ordered, Kate began, "Do you mind if we rehash what we think we have?"

Colm took out his notebook and flicked through before coming to rest at a page filled with writing, and looked up expectantly.

"Our first problem is establishing the murder scene. Was our victim killed at the house or lured out to the field? And in both cases how did she get there?"

Colm looked pensive, "I can't see a woman of her intelligence, or her age, come to that, being lured to the field. I think the house is our murder scene."

Kate nodded her agreement. "But how did our murderer move the body? In the original investigation mispers ruled out any car or taxi hire."

"And the PA says she would have heard any movement on the gravel because her room is at the front."

"What about the back?"

Colm looked quizzical, "Back?"

"We haven't checked if there is rear access to the garden. I'd assumed the gardener took things down the side of the house but what if there is a back way?" Kate pulled her own notebook out and jotted down. Something to check on Monday.

"We've still got the problem of how they actually moved her. A dead weight is just that - bodies are heavy even when a small build and Grace was not stick thin, according to her publicity photographs, and those are normally airbrushed, aren't they?"

"I certainly don't think a woman on her own could move her but I think a man could, even if he struggled a bit."

Their conversation ceased as their food was brought to the table. Both had opted for a classic burger and chips, although Colm had gone for the half pounder. For a few minutes they both concentrated on their food. Kate cut hers in half before picking it up to eat. Colm took his in both hands and chomped down with determination. A few mouthfuls later he said, "We've got plenty of motives but what if our murderer isn't someone who was at the party but someone else Grace was blackmailing?"

Kate wiped her mouth and swallowed. "And we have the anonymous letter writer. Was he or she out to teach her a lesson? Hoping she'd reform."

Colm put his half-eaten burger on the plate and took a deep drink of cola. "And when she didn't he or she killed her?"

Kate nodded. "We still don't have enough information. We have the broad outline but no details." She looked and felt despondent.

Colm added to her gloom, "And, of course, we have people lying to us. The PA is still not coming clean about something and neither are our two actors here."

"And now we learn that the solicitor wasn't too happy with our victim on the night of the murder, which he failed to mention."

"Well, it could be worse and we could have reached a blind alley with nowhere to turn. At least we have information to follow up on. And forensics may come back with something on the money in our victim's account and the letters."

"True. Come on then, eat up and we'll head for home."

CHAPTER 42

Kate had arrived back in plenty of time to have a bath and meet up with Jude and her friends. The problem was she was no longer sure she wanted to go. The naysayer's voice was drowning out Siobhan's encouragement. Now, she stood outside the Crown and Gown trying to build up the courage to go in.

In June it wasn't dark yet and Kate stood to one side and peered through the window. Immediately, she caught sight of Jude and three other women, all of them looking younger than Kate. Jude seemed at ease and laughter followed a comment she had made to the group. Then she was standing up and collecting glasses prior to going to the bar for another round.

The other women looked friendly enough but it was clear that they all knew one another. Kate didn't get the impression that Jude was with anyone of them especially but would she, Jude, really want to babysit Kate all evening? Would she feel honour bound to stay with Kate all the time? Kate wouldn't mind that but she didn't want to be a nuisance.

Jude returned from the bar with a tray and set drinks before her friends. Kate was just about to take her courage in her hands when a fifth woman joined the group, but not before she had come up beside Jude and planted a sloppy kiss on her cheek. Far from looking surprised, Jude seemed pleased and jumped up and hugged the new arrival, warmly. She was of a similar age to Jude, perhaps a little younger, but not by much and it was clear that there was something special between the two of them.

Kate stopped and observed. The new arrival pulled up a chair from another table and placed herself close to Jude. The two of them had their heads together and were ignoring the other women, who in turn, seemed to expect this action. Kate's heart sank. Far from there being a spark between her and Jude, she saw now that Jude was just being kind. That was her decision made. If Jude was going to be busy with her lover she wouldn't want to be looking out for Kate. That wouldn't be fair.

Turning away, Kate walked back towards the high street. She could either catch a bus or pop into the taxi office next door to the bus stop. Kate had to be honest, although disappointed that Jude was already in a relationship, she was relieved not to be going out with a group of women she didn't know. "And never would know if she kept running away!" said Siobhan's voice. She tried to placate the voice by arguing that it would not have been fair on Jude if she had gone in. She was just trying to be fair. Siobhan's response was a loud raspberry. Kate smiled to herself. That was Siobhan's normal response if she'd been out-argued. Before she forgot, she texted a short message to Jude, "Sorry. Tied up with work. See you at the gym one morning?"

◆ ◆ ◆

Mid-morning on the Sunday Kate was busy in her role as homemaker. The washing was in the machine. She'd changed her bed. Put her hoover round and marvelled at the fur pile Monster left in his now nightly position by the chair. Once she'd put the sheets on the line she would go to the supermarket and shop for the week ahead. She might even get some fresh produce and make something to heat up later in the week.

Her thoughts were interrupted by her mobile ringing. She hurried through to the lounge where she had left it charging. She sincerely hoped it wasn't work. It wasn't. It was Jude. Kate was in two minds about answering but common sense prevailed. "Hi Jude. How was your evening?"

"Good. Sorry you didn't make it. I think you would have loved it."

"Another time perhaps?"

"Yes sure. Look, are you free today? Now? Do you fancy a drink? Not alcohol, obviously."

"I was off to the supermarket in a minute. I need to shop for the week ahead because I rarely get time when I'm working."

"Are you going to the one on the Westergate

Road?"

"Err, yes."

"How about a coffee in their café? I could do with doing some food shopping myself."

Kate's heart was beating erratically. What would Jude's lover say about them meeting up? Common sense tried to rear its head. Friends can have a coffee together. And now she knew Jude was in a relationship that would be how she would behave. "That would be lovely. What time were you thinking?"

"An hour?"

Kate quickly did a mental calculation involving washing machine cycle, her own need to shower and getting there. "Yes. An hour would be great. See you in there."

"Lovely. See you later." The phone went down and Kate moved into haste mode.

CHAPTER 43

Kate was there early and debated between waiting in her car for the correct moment or going in and finding a table. She opted for the latter and then found that Jude had been even earlier. She was already sat at a table with a coffee in front of her. She rose as Kate approached. "Latte? Anything to eat?"

"A latte, yes. But I can get mine," Kate attempted to shoo Jude back into her seat but she was already heading towards the counter.

Kate made herself comfortable at the table and watched as Jude chatted with the counter server and then made her way back to their table with a cup in hand. She smiled broadly. "I'm glad you could make today."

Kate smiled, "Me too."

They both sipped their drinks and then smiled at one another. Then Jude took a deep breath, "I saw you last night. At the Crown and Gown. Why didn't you come in? I thought at one point you were going to and then you didn't."

Kate felt herself blushing furiously. It started at the base of her neck and rose in one single wave to her forehead. "I err..." What the hell should she say? Siobhan's voice again, *the truth.* "I suddenly felt out of place and I thought... I thought you wouldn't want to be looking out for me all evening."

Jude put her head on one side and stared at Kate. "Do you think I hadn't already thought about that? If it was going to be a problem I wouldn't have asked you."

Kate looked at the froth on her coffee rather than meet Jude's gaze. "I'm sorry. I just got cold feet."

Jude grinned. "I understand that. How about if I tell you about who you would have met last night?"

"Okay." Well this would be one way of having her thoughts about the late arrival last night confirmed.

"If you imagine I'm sat at twelve o'clock, then on my left at about two was Kylie. She's the youngest of the group and only joins us when she's down from university. At five there was Shaz. She works in an office." Jude rubbed her nose. "To be honest I'm not really sure what she does. I must ask her."

"She looked like a youngster as well."

"Yes, I think she's only a few years older than Kylie. Then at seven and nine you had Anya and Sammie. They're a couple. They both work for the distribution warehouse out at the Waterly Cross estate. Anya drives lorries."

"Was she the one with the short bob haircut?"

"Yes. She doesn't look big enough does she? But she's a tough nut despite her size."

Kate was worried that Jude had finished the thumbnail character descriptions.

"And the woman who came in late?" She hoped she sounded interested and that her face reflected this emotion.

"Oh yes, Susie. She's a force to be reckoned with!" Jude gave an affectionate laugh. "She's probably my best friend and certainly my oldest. We met in nursery and have been friends ever since. Even though we went to different schools and she went to uni we can just pick up like we only spoke yesterday. Do you know what I mean?"

Kate nodded her understanding. That was just how she and Siobhan were. It was good to have a friend like that.

"The only downside is that she's straight!" Jude laughed. "No, seriously, she's married with kids but sometimes comes out with us. She says she likes the safety of the women only spaces we go to."

Kate raised an eyebrow, "Doesn't her husband mind?"

Jude looked surprised, "Why should he? Susie's perfectly safe with us."

Kate stopped her next comment. Why should he mind? She was making stereotypical observations about someone she'd never met. It infuriated her when people did that about gay people so she'd better rethink her attitude.

There was a few seconds of, what Kate felt

was uncomfortable silence, before Jude said, "Look, perhaps a night out at a disco wasn't the best thing to invite you to for your first chance of meeting people. What are you like at pub quizzes?"

Kate was surprised. "Pub quizzes? I don't know. It's not something I've ever tried. Isn't it all middle aged people, or older?"

Jude laughed again and Kate decide she liked her laugh. It was deep and soft and made Kate unconsciously smile in response.

"It's an easy going quiz, no one takes it too seriously and the ages range from old enough to drink through to old enough to remember the good old days!"

Kate smiled at the description. "I don't have any specialised knowledge. I imagine you're good at sports?"

Jude nodded. "Yes, some but I also like history and they're not Mastermind questions, just good general knowledge. Do you want to come?"

Did she want to go? That was a leading question. Who else would be there? Didn't Jude have an established team? She put all these questions to Jude, who explained that the team varied in size from three to six, depending on who was free and so Kate's presence was unlikely to be a problem.

"Anya and Sammie will be there. Then we have a choice of Cathy, who works shifts at a nursing home and Clive and Kev from my place. I'm not sure what shifts they're working this week." Kate still hesitated and Jude took the initiative again. "It's tomorrow at The Mitre. How about I come and pick you up and then you don't have to enter a strange place on your own?"

Kate thought, Susie was a friend and she was being given a second chance to get to know this woman who, she admitted to herself, she was becoming more and more attracted to. She smiled to herself, she knew what Siobhan would be saying.

Jude took the smile as affirmation, "I'll pick you up about seven tomorrow? Where do you live?"

Kate was swept along by her positivity and gave her address, "As long as you accept that I might, genuinely, have to cry off if something urgent comes up at work."

"No problem."

They both looked at the dregs of their coffees and Jude said, "Okay, I'd better get my bits and pieces and get sorted for the week ahead." She stood and smiled at Kate.

"I'm glad you said yes, both to the coffee and the quiz. See you tomorrow."

And with a parting smile, she left.

CHAPTER 44

Kate had slept well and managed an hour at the gym, although she didn't see Jude. Now she was sat at her desk in the incident room waiting for her colleagues to arrive. The office had been stuffy after being closed through a warm night and she had thrown the windows wide open to allow the cooler air of the early morning to draw in.

Once again she looked through her notes from the previous week and confirmed the list of tasks she and her team would need to complete that she'd drawn up the previous night. Switching her computer on she wondered whether forensics had been able to get anything useful from the letter. The short answer was no. There had been two distinct sets of prints and by sending a constable to the victim's house they had been able to identify both sets. One was, as Kate had expected, Josephine Grace's and the other, also no surprise, Gordon Delver's.

The only interesting finds were that the rough edges of the paper, where it had been torn from the notepad, had deposits on them. Forensics had identified pale blue threads. Several samples of local soil and black carbon. Mike had added quite a complicated report for these deposits but also, thank goodness, a layman's explanation. In short the black carbon was soot and probably from somewhere that was still using traditional coal. The colour and composition were very different from modern smokeless fuels.

Kate's thoughts were broken in on by her awareness of a heavy tread making its way up the stairs. She was pretty sure that was Len and the lighter, faster step was Alice. Just as Len had reached the office door, Kate heard the solid fast beat of Colm's step. Always taking the stairs at a run. Salutations exchanged Kate began to talk to her team as they sat and switched on their computers.

She relayed the information from forensics about the letters and her and Colm's visit to London. She then addressed Len, "Where have we got to with the caterers and musicians?"

Len turned to the room, "Caterers are clear. They used the staff they always do. They thought it had been a lovely evening. No-one getting too drunk, no arguments, no pinched bottoms," Len looked up from his notes, "apparently that's a hazard for the girls. I'm still tracking down the musicians."

Kate nodded and turned to Alice, "Anything back from Zara?"

"Yes, she traced those two strange payments to our victim's account." She paused as she perused the information on her screen and then, "One's from Richard Salisbury and the other

Gerald Purcell."

"Bugger!" Colm blew out.

"I'll give them bugger!" Kate was seriously frustrated. She turned to Colm. "Get them both on the phone and tell them I expect to see them in our interview room no later than three this afternoon. You might also want to convey the impression that they maybe wise to bring their solicitors with them." Kate ran her fingers through her hair; and decided she needed to wash it. She knew they'd been hiding something. Well, she'd make them squirm now. She would not be messed with.

"What if they say they don't have time if they're working?" Colm asked.

Kate smiled thinly, "I checked, they don't do Monday performances. I want them here and you can also convey how seriously pissed off I am!" Kate blew out harshly and took a slow breath in before she continued. "Are they still paying, Alice?"

Alice rapidly clicked through several screens before replying, "They both made their last payment December 2015."

Kate looked thoughtful, "So they paid until they thought she wasn't coming back."

"Or thought it would look odd if they stopped paying after she immediately disappeared," suggested Colm.

"Another question we need to ask them. Right, here's what we need to do today. There seem to be a number of people who are being economical with the truth in this case, so Colm, you and I are going back to see the PA and, if he's still there, the solicitor. We'll also check on a back entrance." Kate explained to Alice and Len about trying to tie down where the murder had taken place and how their victim got to the field.

"Len, I'd like you to do a double check of the car hire places and look for anyone on the cast and technical crew that may have hired a vehicle in the week around the time of our victim's surmised murder." Kate watched as Len made notes and nodded his understanding. She continued, "Also can you do a check on Will Miller?" A frown appeared on Len's face at the name. It was not one that had come up before. "He's the gardener at the Grace house. He's probably fine but let's not leave any stone unturned." Len nodded.

Kate moved on to Alice. "I want you to see if you can confirm the accusations in the letters, especially the woman whose baby our victim is said to have sold and the child itself."

Alice moved across to take the copies of the letters and Kate continued, "It's going to take some digging because I am sure we aren't the first to try and find out what Grace was up to between '67 and '71 but we do have the advantage of a name."

Alice nodded and moved back to her desk, "Colm, if you contact our lying duo, I'll meet you in the car park in fifteen."

Colm nodded and one hand was already reaching for his desk phone while the other clicked through the information on his screen. Kate left. She would quickly pop in to forensics and thank both Mike and Zara for their weekend work. She knew how snowed under they were and she appreciated them going the extra mile for her and her team.

CHAPTER 45

Kate was pleased to see that the solicitor's car was still parked on Grace's drive. It was several minutes before their knock was answered and it was clearly written on Claire Bayntry's face and in her tone of voice that she was not pleased to see them. "Oh! Inspector. How may I help you?"

"Good morning Ms Bayntry. Is Mr Delver available?"

Relief flooded her face, "Yes. Please come in." She held the door wide and then closed it behind them. Leading the way, she said, "He's going through Josey's papers in her study." Stopping before the door, she knocked before opening it. "Gordon, the police are here again."

Kate heard but did not see Gordon Delver's welcome. Bayntry stepped aside and allowed Kate and Colm to enter. Just as she was closing the door, Kate leaned back and asked, "Would you be available for a few more questions later?" Although phrased as a question, the PA understood the underlying message and nodded her acceptance.

Gordon Delver was behind a large wooden, antique desk. He had stood at their entry and now shook each of them warmly by the hand. "Any news?"

Kate shook her head. "No, I'm sorry. We're

here to ask a few more questions."

"Ah! Please take a seat." He sat himself and moved a pile of papers to one side so that he could rest his forearms on the desk. He looked at them intently.

Kate began. "We have been interviewing everyone who attended Ms Grace's party that evening and we have been told that you were not on good terms with Ms Grace that evening."

Delver played for time. He leant back in his chair and pulled at his cuffs. Kate was about to push when he began, "To start with I was just Josey's legal representative but over time I became more like her steward, in the old sense of the word." He looked at Kate for her understanding. She nodded. "One of my tasks was to gather the various documents needed for her annual tax returns and pass them on to the accountant we use." He paused. His eyes searched the bookshelves behind where Kate sat before he focused on her again. "The year Josey disappeared I received a perplexing call from the accountant to say that there were discrepancies in Josey's finances. The main one being that she appeared to have spent more than she earned for the previous year."

"Could she explain that?"

"That was the issue of our disagreement. I had tried to talk to Josey about it on the telephone but she was uncharacteristically obtuse. In fact the only reason I attended the blessed party was so that I could talk with her face to face."

"Did you manage to do that on the night of the party?"

Delver sighed deeply. "No, she claimed she was too busy when I first arrived and then of course the party was underway and it wasn't the time or place for such a discussion."

"Couldn't you have waited until the end of the evening?"

"I did consider it but I knew I would be tired and irritable and Josey would be," a pause and a delicate cough, "merry!"

Kate waited and was rewarded. "What I said before was true. I was very tired and decided to go to bed early, planning to talk with Josey on the Saturday." Silence descended as Delver thought back to that night. He gave a hollow laugh, "I even thought, when we couldn't find Josey the following day that she was deliberately avoiding our conversation." His eyes teared up. "If only we'd known."

"Did you have any idea where Josey had got the extra money from?" Colm interceded.

Again, a gathering silence before Delver answered. "At the time, no. But since the revelations in those letters I can only assume she was using..." Kate could see the visible struggle going on in Delver's mind. "I suppose it was blackmail money." He finished in a lower voice. "I had hoped to find an explanation amongst these," he indicated the piles of papers, "but nothing explains the extra money."

Kate rose. Although she couldn't definitively rule him out she didn't think the solicitor was their murderer. As she turned to go she did ask, "And you still didn't hear anything in the middle of the night?"

Delver shook his head wistfully. "I wish I had. Perhaps I would have been able to stop her death." He rose as he said this and again shook their hands. "You will let me know when you have any news, won't you."

"Thank you sir, we will do our best."

Kate and Colm left with Colm pulling the door quietly behind him. "That's one disillusioned man."

Kate agreed. "Come on. We need to have another chat with the PA."

CHAPTER 46

Kate made her way to the back of the house and through to the kitchen. Claire Bayntry wasn't there. As she was about to turn away she spied her in the garden, talking to Will Miller. They were gazing at a bit of grass below the conservatory and the gardener was sketching something in a small notebook. Kate and Colm walked out to meet them.

"Good morning Mr Miller. Great plans ahead?"

"Good morning Inspector Medlar. Mr Delver thought that having a patio here might enhance the garden and the house." He showed her his rough sketch. Kate saw the bare outline of the house and the garden shape and then a curved design that linked the conservatory to the side path.

"That looks lovely. Will you do it or will you get someone in?"

Miller laughed. "Jack of all trades me. I can do a patio. Did you need to talk with me or can I get on?"

"Just one question: does this garden have a rear access point?"

"Will nodded and then pointed to a shrubbery, "Behind there is a gate to the lane that runs behind all these houses. It's only wide enough for one vehicle but it does mean we can bring things directly into the garden."

"Thank you." Kate turned to the PA, "Ms Bayntry may we have a few words, please?"

Bayntry nodded and led them back towards the kitchen. Kate turned back from following, to ask, "Do you own a car Mr Miller."

Miller laughed. "On my wages and doing up the cottage, a vehicle is a luxury. I have my bike."

"What about when you buy stuff, for here or your cottage?"

"Most places do deliveries. It's not a problem."

Kate turned back to follow Colm and Bayntry leaving Miller to pace out the design of the new patio.

Sat once again at the kitchen table, Kate began, determined that she was going to get the truth from Claire Bayntry. "Ms Bayntry, would you talk us through the evening of the party again?"

"Again?"

"You see we have interviewed a great many people and your account doesn't quite tally with others." A bit of a stretch of the truth but she needed to lean a little.

"Oh." Her tone was not one of surprise. She began again to detail the evening from the point at which Josephine Grace had returned home to her own retirement to bed.

Kate and Colm sat impassively. "What about

anyone who appeared out or sorts or not their usual self with Ms Grace?"

Bayntry opened her mouth as if to reply glibly but Colm prevented her, "Please remember we have accumulated a great deal of information and are now cross-referencing it all."

That caused Bayntry to pause and then her shoulders sagged a little. She made eye contact with Kate, "You mean Gordon and Josey being cross with one another, don't you?"

Kate waited and Bayntry sighed. "I only didn't tell you because I didn't want you to think Gordon was involved. He was as shocked as I was when we couldn't find Josey the following day."

Kate still waited and the PA hastened to fill the silence. "I didn't know what they had argued about but I'd heard Josey's end of a telephone conversation a few days before the party and then she avoided Gordon all evening and he didn't look very happy."

"What did you assume the problem was?"

"I didn't really know. Josey had said something about Gordon being too anxious and that it was easily explained but I have no idea what it was about."

Kate and Colm waited and Bayntry was eager to fill the gap. "Josey could be very... mercurial at times. She could be hard to pin down if you needed a definitive answer. I just thought Gordon was trying to get her to make a decision and Josey was putting it off."

Somewhere in the house a telephone rang. Bayntry jumped up. "Please excuse me. I'm expecting a call from the estate agent about a visit." Not waiting for an answer, she rushed off.

"Do you think there's something going on between her and the solicitor?" Colm speculated.

Kate gave it some thought. "There might be a crush on her part but I didn't get the impression that Delver was looking to replace his wife."

CHAPTER 47

Bayntry returned, full of apologies and hesitated at the table as though unsure whether she needed to sit again. Kate indicated the chair and she sat. Kate thanked her for the information just shared and then continued, "Could you remind us of the noise you heard at two-fifteen that night?"

Colm made a show of checking through his notebook. He wanted to remind her that they had an awful lot of information and that she needed to be totally honest with them.

This time Bayntry didn't rush to fill the gap. She closed her eyes and breathed in deeply before blowing out in one stream. "I know how this is going to look but I did it for the best of reasons."

Kate's neck prickled. Were they finally getting somewhere? Kate saw a line of perspiration form across Bayntry's top lip and a droplet run along the edge of her hairline.

"Did you hear a noise?"

Bayntry nodded.

"And did you investigate the noise?"

Another nod. Kate and Colm waited. Trying to curb their impatience.

"I did think it was a door closing but it sounded like the kitchen door. It is a very heavy old door and makes a very deep sound when it's closed. And you can't shut it quietly because you need to lift and pull sharply."

"So you decided to check what had caused the noise?"

"Not immediately. I thought it was Josey locking up and so waited to hear her come up. When she didn't, I went to find her."

"How long did you wait?"

"I don't really know. Five minutes?"

"Where did you go?"

"I was going to check the kitchen but there was only a light showing in the front lounge. I went in." The PA gave a shudder as the memory resurfaced in her mind. "Josey was sat in the armchair by the fire." She appealed to Kate, "I thought she was asleep and went to shake her to get her to bed." She shook her head. "But she was dead. I could see that she'd been strangled. There were red marks all around her neck. I didn't know what to do."

Genuinely perplexed, Kate asked, "Why not call the police?"

"I know I should have done but... You see I was worried that the blame would fall on Gordon, because he and Josey had argued and was unhappy that night." She hastened to add, "I knew he hadn't but I thought it might look bad for him."

"How could you be so sure it wasn't Mr Delver?" Colm asked.

Bayntry shrugged. "I just knew and he

was genuinely horrified and confused when we couldn't find Josey the following morning."

"So, what did you do with the body?"

Bayntry's face was a picture of horror. "I didn't move her!" She looked shocked that they would think such a thing. "I left her there and thought I would pretend to find her in the morning."

"How would that stop us from thinking Mr Delver had a hand in her death?"

Bayntry blushed. "I unlocked all the doors so that it looked like anyone could have come in during the night."

"What did you think when her body wasn't there in the morning?"

"I didn't know what to think. I even persuaded myself that I had dreamt it and that when I went up with Josey's tea she would be in bed."

"Were all the doors locked when you went to open them all? Including the kitchen door?"

Bayntry nodded. "Yes."

"So, whoever killed and then moved the body must have a key to the house. Probably the kitchen key."

Bayntry's mouth gaped open. "I hadn't thought of that. Oh my God!"

"Who has keys to the house?"

"Me, Josey and Gordon." Her face paled and she suddenly looked pinched. "I didn't do it. Honest. And I'm sure Gordon didn't either. He's not that kind of man."

A burglar who left no sign of a forced entry? And then Kate reminded herself that Bayntry had opened all the doors so the misper investigation would not have looked for such signs.

"What about Ms Grace's keys?"

"They were found in her handbag, along with her purse and cards."

"I don't suppose you checked her handbag when you found her body?"

Bayntry shook her head. "I left everything as I found it. Apart from checking that Josey was dead, I didn't touch anything."

Kate rose. "Ms Bayntry I need you to come to the station and make a formal statement. You are very lucky that I'm not charging you with obstruction. Your editing of the truth had left us unable to even decide where the murder scene was." Kate allowed her frustration to show through. "Colm I'll call for a car. Would you take Ms Bayntry back to the station? I'm going to see Ms Cullen."

Colm nodded and made himself more comfortable in his chair and Kate left to radio her instructions from the car.

CHAPTER 48

Having organised for a car to pick up Colm and Claire Bayntry, Kate got in touch with her office. Alice picked up on the third ring. Kate began, "Can you book an interview room for Colm? He's coming in with the PA to take a formal statement."

"Will do. Salisbury and Purcell rang back and confirmed that they would attend the station this afternoon. Neither made any mention of bringing a solicitor."

"Thank you. Would you ask Len to add Will Miller to his list of names of those who may have hired a vehicle? I'm off to see Tamara Cullen and then I'll be in. Anything else?"

"Bart, sorry boss, DCI Bartholomew has asked that you give him a debrief at some point today but it's not urgent."

"Right. Oh, Alice," a thought had just occurred to her, "can you find out from Traffic how long they keep their camera footage for." It was a long shot but they might keep it for years. Could they then trace a vehicle from the back of their victim's house?

Having finished with the office, Kate contacted Tamara Cullen and confirmed that she was home. Kate estimated that it would take her about fifteen minutes to get there and maybe it would have if there hadn't been roadworks on the one way system. Having followed diversion after diversion, Kate pulled over and inputted the address into the satnav. It, at least, would cope with the diversions.

Twenty minutes later Kate pulled up on an estate of new houses. Cullen lived in a three-storey block of flats, which Kate guessed had been part of the affordable housing clause in the planning permission. Although the building looked no bigger than a three-storey house, Kate noted from the buzzer list that it contained six flats. Cullen lived on the ground floor and the opening click came almost simultaneously with Kate's push on the buzzer.

Walking in, Kate caught the faint aroma of fresh paint. These flats were really new. The door of number two was open and a delicate young woman hovered in the doorway. "Ms Cullen?"

"Oh, yes. Detective Medlar?" She held out a hand and Kate shook it. It was a little limp and clung a little too long. Kate didn't bother with correcting the inaccuracy of the title. A little breathlessly, the woman continued, "Do come in."

Kate followed Cullen into, probably the smallest flat she had ever seen. The door opened immediately into the front room and an archway revealed the kitchen. Kate had seen bigger spaces on board a yacht. Two chairs, a television and a desk filled the room. Cullen sat in one chair and indicated Kate should take the second.

Before Kate had fully seated herself, Cullen jumped up again, "I should offer you a drink?"

Kate indicated that Cullen sit, "I'm fine thank you. I just need to ask some follow up questions."

Cullen sat and nervously twisted her fingers, watching Kate much as a mouse fearing a pouncing cat. Kate tried to put her at her ease. "This is a lovely flat. Have you been here long?"

Cullen shook her head. "I only moved in five weeks ago. It's okay. But at least it's mine." Her right leg had begun to quiver.

Kate was unsure what was making her so nervous and thought it best to just get on with her questions. "When my colleagues questioned you last week they felt that perhaps you had more to say but were unsure whether it was relevant."

The woman dropped her eyes and Kate continued. "Anything you say maybe of vital importance. If it isn't, that's fine, you won't be wasting our time. We need to hear the information and see if it helps us. You do want us to catch Ms Grace's killer, don't you?"

"Oh yes," somewhat breathlessly.

"So," Kate said, adopting a coaxing tone, "what had you thought of that you weren't sure was relevant?"

The fingers continued to twist and the leg continued to tremble. "It only happened the once but I thought Josey looked upset."

"What happened?"

"Well," deep breath, "A lot of fan mail gets delivered to the station and it's Vanessa's job to sort and open it. If a letter is marked personal, she doesn't open it and leaves it on top of the pile." This was said almost in one breath and now she breathed deeply again. "One day, I came across Josey in one of the rehearsal rooms going through her mail. Well, in fact not going through her mail. She was staring at one letter in her hand and she had gone an awful colour. I asked her if she was okay and she seemed to shake herself and smiled and said she was fine. But I could see that whatever was in that letter had really upset her."

"When was this?"

"I don't know exactly but it must have been around Valentine's Day because some of her mail was cards."

"The February of the year she was murdered?"

"No," a pause and thought, "No. I'm pretty sure it was the year before."

"What did the letter look like?"

Cullen looked at Kate as though she were mad, "Look like?"

"The colour of the paper. A4 paper, smaller, larger?" Kate explained patiently.

"Oh. Of course." Time for thought. "It was like paper from a spiral bound notepad. The top of the paper still showed where it had been ripped off. So it was smaller than A4 and it was just the one sheet."

"Did you see an envelope?"

"There was an ordinary white one on the desk in front of Josey. I assumed the letter had been marked private or personal."

"Did Ms Grace ever refer to that letter, or similar letters again to you?"

Cullen shook her head vigorously. "No, never. I think she was embarrassed that I had seen her reaction to that one."

Kate thanked Cullen for her time and left. So that answered the question of how their victim had received the letters. She checked the time. She just had enough time to go and have a chat with Vanessa at REAl Radio.

CHAPTER 49

Vanessa had little to add to the information Cullen had provided. She couldn't identify the letters. Yes, if they were marked as private or personal, she left them for the cast to open. No, she didn't remember any distinctive envelopes or handwriting. At that time their victim was getting twenty or thirty letters each day. How could she, Vanessa, remember them all?

Leaving REAl Radio, Kate sat in her car and tried to coalesce the information she had gained over the last few hours. They now knew that death was around two in the morning. The murderer may have a key to the house, or more likely she or he had borrowed the victim's keys and then didn't need them to leave a second time because the PA had opened all the doors. The garden had rear access and so the murderer could have moved the body to a vehicle in the back lane. It was unlikely anyone would have been around at that time of the night.

She had plenty of people with motive but, as of yet, no-one who had the means. She turned the key in the ignition. Perhaps Len and Alice had more news. She'd better also pop in and talk to Bart. Not that they were any closer to identifying the killer. Kate's frustration spiked. What hadn't she noticed on Friday? And where did they go from here?

On the way back to the station Kate picked up coffee and cakes. She and her team needed a team briefing; share whatever little bits and pieces they had acquired.

Entering the office, she called out, "Team meeting in five, please." She received various affirmations.

Once murmurs of appreciation had died down, Kate began. "Today, we have been able to confirm both the site of the murder and the time: in the lounge of our victim's home at about two in the morning. We have two lines of investigation. No, make that three. Firstly, Josephine Grace was in the habit of blackmailing some of her acquaintances. However, all those we know of do not have the opportunity or the means of carrying out the murder."

Kate turned to Len, "Where have you got to with the hiring of vehicles?"

Len shook his head, downbeat. "I've even gone to a thirty mile radius, and no-one that we have on our list hired any vehicle around the time of the murder."

"Right. Secondly, we have the phantom letter writer, *Your Conscience*. Alice, where have you got to with that?"

Alice took up a sheaf of papers and began to deliver her findings. "I found Sylvie Hardcastle; well what I mean is I was able to track her life. During the time she was with Melissa Smith, who doesn't appear on the electoral list, she lived in a house in Putney. I tracked down the address and had a look at her neighbours. There's one woman, Barbara Hawkes, who lived there until a few years ago. She's about the same age as our victim so I think she's still alive. I can't find a death certificate for her. She may know more about Melissa and Sylvie. Perhaps even what happened to the baby."

"That's a bit of a long shot, isn't it?" Colm queried.

Kate agreed but there again, they were out of other leads. "Did you find out where Sylvie died?"

Alice shook her head. "You know how tight patient records are."

"What about the traffic footage?"

Alice looked glum. "Sorry boss," she made it sound like she was personally to blame, "but the purely traffic ones only keep their recordings for a matter of hours and CCTV tends to be ninety days maximum and some are only thirty."

"Wouldn't the original misper team have looked at that?" Colm asked.

Kate shrugged. She knew she was clutching at straws. "I knew it was a long shot."

Colm ran his thoughts past them. "From the sound of it the letter writer was watching our victim. He, I still think it is a he, comments about Grace taking up with the young people and how down in the mouth Gifford is. So he must have had her under surveillance. Surely someone would notice if the same person is hanging around either outside the house or at the radio station?"

Kate brightened, "A very good point. Len I want you to go back through public contacts and see if anyone from 2013 to 2015 reported anyone acting suspiciously; or the same car always being parked where it wasn't known; you know the sort of thing I mean." Len nodded as he made notes.

"Colm, tomorrow, go back to the radio station and ask Vanessa and anyone else who is a regular visitor to the station, if they noticed anyone hanging around in the same time period. You know what to ask for." Colm nodded his agreement.

Kate then turned to Alice. A plan had been fermenting at the back of her mind as they'd talked for the last few minutes. "How do you fancy a day in London tomorrow?" Alice's face lit up. "I'll have a word with Bart about letting the Met know I'm going to be on their patch."

"So we're going to find Barbara Hawkes?"

"That's the plan. If you can sort out directions for getting to her old address. Let's hope someone in her street knows where she disappeared to. Perhaps sheltered accommodation."

As Alice and Len returned to their work stations Kate addressed Colm. "How did it go with Bayntry?"

Colm nodded, "Fine. There were more tears and remonstrations about her and Delver's innocence."

"What's your thought?"

Colm looked pensive before replying. "It makes sense and yet I can't see either of them having the stomach for it. And we still have the problem about how they moved the body."

"She could have used her own car and lied about not hearing any vehicles on the drive," Kate suggested.

"No. Loving's car was parked in front of the garage. How did they move that? Loving's not likely to have left her keys lying around."

"She might have. Double check tomorrow. I know it's another long shot." Kate checked her watch. "I've just got time to update Bart and okay another London trip. Then we'll go and meet our lying actors."

CHAPTER 50

It took Kate longer than she thought it would to convince Detective Chief Inspector Bartholomew that following information gleaned from the anonymous letters was a valid lead. Finally, he agreed to let the local force in Putney know that she would be in their area and a contact name in case she had need of official help. Rushing back into the office she saw Colm put his desk phone down and nod her way, "Our actors are here, sans solicitors and asking to speak with us together."

"That's not going to happen! I am sure they've rehearsed their lines anyway. They don't need one another's support. They may just forget their script if we separate them."

Colm grinned. "I thought you might say that so I asked the desk sergeant to put them in separate rooms."

"Do you want to take Alice in with you and I'll take Len?"

Colm looked surprised but pleased, "Yeh, sure!"

"Who do you want?"

Colm gave it some thought, "I'll take Salisbury."

Kate nodded her affirmation and then called Alice and Len across. "Do you want some interviewing experience?"

They both nodded enthusiastically. "Okay, here's the rule. You don't say anything, other than identifying yourself for the tape. If you have a brainwave, write it down and slip it to me or Colm. Understood?"

Both returned to their desks and picked up paper and pen. "Right, Len you're with me and we're interviewing Gerald Purcell. He was at the party but went back to The Grand after with Richard Salisbury. They came by train and according to all your searches they didn't hire a vehicle so we have the problem about how they or he transported the body. They lied about their relationship with our victim and we know that they were paying money to her on a monthly basis."

Everyone nodded their assimilation of the facts and Kate led her team down to the interview rooms. Colm and Alice peeled off to the first room and Kate and Len entered the second. Gerald Purcell was hunched over the table, the fingers of his right hand tapping the scratched surface. As Kate sat down, he sat up straight, crossed his left leg over his right and portrayed a man at ease.

For the tape, Kate introduced herself, Len and Purcell and repeated that he could have access to a solicitor if he wished. He forewent his right to legal representation and Kate began.

"Mr Purcell, when we interviewed you in your flat you said that your relationship with

Josephine Grace was one of friendship and yet each month you were paying her a sizeable sum of money. Was she blackmailing you?" Kate noticed a twitch at the corner of his right eye. Had he not expected them to find out about the money?

Purcell looked Kate straight in the eye, "Yes she was blackmailing me."

"And Mr Salisbury?"

"Yes, and Dickie."

"So far from being on friendly terms you have a motive for wanting her dead."

Purcell took in a deep breath and leaned forward slightly, "We did not kill Josey."

"So, why were you at her party, if she was blackmailing you?"

"Dickie and I had decided that we weren't going to pay any longer. We accepted her invite to the party with the intention of telling her so. That's why we stayed on Friday night. We could have arranged to travel back on the last train."

"Perhaps you did meet with her and she laughed in your face. That must have made you angry. Angry enough to kill."

"If we had met with her and if she had laughed in my face, Dickie and I had already agreed that we would not be blackmailed any longer. We were going to threaten to tell the public what she was doing."

"Would anyone believe you?"

"Maybe not everyone, but mud sticks,

especially in acting."

"So, you were willing to risk your career and confront her? Why would you do that now? Why not before?"

"I hope, Detective Inspector that this will go no further."

Kate gave her usual response. "If the matter is not pertinent to our investigation then it will not be made public."

Purcell leant back and picked an imaginary fleck of fluff from his trouser leg. His eyes were on his hands, not on Kate or Len. "Dickie and I have been lovers since the early nineties and Josey found out."

"I'm not sure I understand why this is a blackmailing situation."

Another deep breath, "Dickie and I got together when we were young. It was at the time of the AIDS epidemic, so not something you shouted about. Anyway we went our separate ways for a few years and in that time Dickie married. However, when we were filming Faringer we rekindled our relationship and that's when Josey found out."

A moment's silence before he continued. "At first she was lovely. She'd invite me along to sessions with Dickie and his wife and she'd monopolize Cheryl so Dickie and I could talk. Then, when she was no longer needed for the series she turned, like a viper." His distaste was evident in the way his mouth grimaced.

"You have to admit Mr Purcell that you have a very strong motive to kill Ms Grace."

"I understand your thinking, Inspector, but I assure you we did not. As I understand it, Josey's body was moved from her home to a field. How did we get her there? Neither of us owns a car and we came down by train. Dickie was as pissed as the proverbial newt and would have been incapable of driving and I have never learnt. Are you suggesting we hired a taxi?" The smile was bleak.

Kate waited a second and then concluded, "Thank you for your time, Mr Purcell. PC Goodfellow will arrange for a copy of this interview and will ask you to sign it. We will be in touch if anything further occurs to us."

Leaving Len to sort the statement signing, Kate left and walked briskly into the observation room but Colm was already saying similar words to Richard Salisbury.

CHAPTER 51

Colm joined Kate in the observation room, "Did you hear any of that?"

Kate shook her head, "No, I've only just popped in here."

"Right, basically he claims that he and Purcell were lovers in the nineties and then they went their separate way. He thought it was just a one off for him and so *wooed*, his words, his now wife. However, when they met again on the Faringer set, it reignited their relationship. They thought they had been very discreet but somehow Josey found out about it. But she didn't start blackmailing them until she'd left the series."

"That pretty much tallies with what Purcell said."

"Did he also tell you that the only reason they'd agreed to attend the party was so that they could talk with our victim and tell them they weren't going to pay anymore?"

Kate nodded, "Did he say what had prompted their decision?"

"Yes. His children are now of an age when they will understand and he thinks Cheryl suspects there is something going on."

"Did you suggest it actually gives them more motive for wanting her dead?"

"I did. And his response was, I quote, 'My dear boy, I wouldn't kill Josey. I would have killed her career and that would have hurt far more.'"

Kate had to agree. The Josephine Grace she had come to know would have really suffered if her blackmailing had become common knowledge.

"We'll meet with the other two and get their thoughts at what they've heard."

Colm nodded.

◆ ◆ ◆

Colm virtually followed Len and Alice back into the incident room and Kate called them all for a team meeting.

"Okay, what are your thoughts on what you heard in the interview room? Are these two, suspects?"

Len waved his notes around, "Our bloke certainly seemed to have motive. Far easier to knock off the victim than confront her. But...," he paused and looked intent, "but I don't get the feeling he has it in him."

"I know having a car is the stumbling point but what if they hired a car in London, drove it down and got the train back so they had a vehicle that no-one's been able to chase down?" Alice offered.

"Phew, that's a long shot," Colm sighed.

"But one worth exploring. Len try contacting

London based hire companies." Seeing the frown on his face, she continued, "Try places near where they live first. And check under both names. I know Purcell says he doesn't drive but..." she let the implication sink in.

Len sighed deeply but nodded. Alice mouthed across the table, "Sorry!"

"What about knowledge of Eashire?" Colm contributed. "Neither man is a local and I think it would take local knowledge to find that field even if the preservation on the trees was just a lucky chance."

"I agree. But I still don't think we can rule them out definitively."

"What about the fact that Purcell said Salisbury was pissed. He wouldn't have been able to drive even if they had a car," Len added.

"It could all have been an act," Alice intervened. "They're both actors so Salisbury pretends to be drunk, plays up to the hotel porter as a witness and then creeps out the back of the hotel."

"You're certainly one for the conspiracy theories, aren't you?" Len said with a slight sneer.

Before Alice could reply, Kate said, "All scenarios have to be considered, researched and ruled in or out." She stared at Len until he looked away. "So these two have to remain suspects as does Craig Masters."

Len coughed as he hastily swallowed his mouthful, "No, he's clear boss. He rang yesterday to say he thought on that night in August he was working for a band as a roadie and they were playing in North Wales, Bangor Uni."

"You checked?"

"Of course, boss," endeavouring to sound hurt. "I spoke with the band's manager and he confirms that Craig Masters was with them and that they were in Bangor. He even said he could confirm it so well because they'd had problems with their mixer desk and Craig sorted it for them."

Kate sighed, "Right, cross through his name on the board, but we have to leave Salisbury and Purcell up there."

They all looked at the board and then Kate closed the meeting. "Alice, you and I need to work out where we're going tomorrow and the earliest train we can catch. Colm you and Len need to have a day chasing down any threads we haven't covered. We are going to solve this case."

CHAPTER 52

Kate was home in plenty of time for the quiz that evening. It had occurred to her on the way home that it would be more sensible if she picked Jude up, since she didn't drink. She had texted with the suggestion and received an affirmative one back, complete with Jude's address.

Before getting out of her car, she tapped it into the satnav and it told her it was a fifteen minute journey. So she had time for food and a shower.

Monster was waiting in his usual place and paced in front of her as she headed for the front door, chuntering all the way.

"I don't know why you're complaining," Kate said to him, "I'm home earlier than usual!"

By this point Kate's key was in the lock and Monster was stalking round the corner to the back door. Kate shook her head. Who else got nagged by a cat? Not even her own cat!

An hour later saw Kate set off. She had ummed and ahhed about her choice of clothes and opted for comfortable jeans and a light shirt. The black jeans combo was too much for a pub, she had decided. With the satnav Jude's flat was easy to find and Kate was pleased to see that Jude was already waiting on the pavement. She rushed to the door to save Kate trying to park. A manoeuvre that would not be a straightforward operation.Breathlessly Jude strapped herself in, "Parking is impossible around here so I thought I'd wait for you!"

"Thanks. It certainly makes life easier."

Then there was silence and Kate struggled to think of a topic of conversation. "I'm assuming I'm going the right way?" she offered.

With a little laugh, Jude replied, "Sorry, yes. You've not been to The Mitre before?"

Kate smiled, "Pubs are not really my thing, unless they serve hot drinks. I get a bit bored with the same tonic and lime or the occasional cola."

Then began a discussion about why Kate didn't drink. She had suffered an extremely bad case of flu; almost hospitalisation bad and lost her sense of both taste and smell. When they'd returned she no longer liked the taste of alcohol, "And believe me, I went through a range of drinks, convinced I would find one I liked."

"But you didn't?"

Kate shook her head. "Nope! Nothing."

"Take the next right," Jude interrupted, "The Mitre is on the left. There you are."

The Mitre was the epitome of a country pub on the outside; lime washed walls and a creeper of some description climbing the walls and sneaking under the roof tiles. Inside it was cosy. Two small bars either side of the entrance with doors leading through to a garden where Kate could see drinkers enjoying the warmth of the evening.

A shout of welcome was directed their way and Kate noticed a table of smiling faces looking at them.

"Come on," Jude said taking hold of her hand, "I'll introduce you."

◆ ◆ ◆

It had been a pleasant evening. Jude's team mates were very welcoming and Kate realised she hadn't laughed so much in a long time. Even when she'd been with Robyn. The quiz had been fun; as Jude had said, just good general knowledge and Kate didn't feel out of her depth. Driving home they chatted about the evening and the people.

"Did you enjoy yourself?" Jude asked.

"Yes. To be honest, far more than I thought I would. You have some lovely friends."

Jude smiled easily, "Yeh, they're a good crew. They liked you, too."

Kate wasn't sure what to do with that compliment, "Is your road the next one on the left?"

Jude sat up straighter, "Yes. Look," she hesitated, "I would love to ask you in but my flatmate is going to be there and Hayley is not good with…" she faltered. "Well, she's not very welcoming and I don't want to blight what has been a lovely evening. Okay?"

Kate was disappointed but she managed to say, "Of course, no problem."

"Look, a parking space!" Jude pointed out. It was a bit of a trek from Jude's place but Kate dutifully pulled into it. Jude undid her seatbelt and turned in her seat so she was facing Kate. Kate mirrored her actions. Tentatively Jude put out a hand to touch Kate's face, "Honestly, Hayley is a cow!"

Kate smiled, "Okay. I believe you."

"Good," Jude leant forward and Kate smelt the wine on her breath. Very deliberately Jude kissed her lips and then withdrew. It was Kate's turn to lean forward. She too put a hand out but she cupped Jude's head and pulled her in for a deeper kiss. Coming up for air Jude asked, "Can we do this again, sometime soon?"

Kate wasn't sure if she meant the quiz or the kiss but she nodded her assent. Then Jude was climbing out of the car, "I'll text you and arrange something."

Kate sat in her seat and watched the disappearing shadow of Jude as she walked up the street, dipping in and out of the bubbles of light from the street lamps. She turned just once to wave and then the dark swallowed her up and she was gone.

CHAPTER 53

Kate found herself for the second time in a week waiting on the station platform for an early train to London. Like Saturday, the air was cool but there was the promise of a warm day to come. Unlike on Saturday the platform was busy with businessmen and women, homogenous in their dark suits and briefcases. There were also the denim hues of students, finding it cheaper to live at home and travel to college rather than pay for accommodation near their university.

Alice had slipped across to the other platform where the coffee kiosk stood and was now descending the stairs with two steaming cups. Kate sniffed appreciatively at the lid as Alice passed her a cup across. Today, Kate had opted for a leather rucksack bag she had treated herself to. Large enough to take the case file and easy enough to carry. Alice too had a rucksack, which hung slackly from her shoulder.

Once on board, Kate and Alice sat side by side for Alice to update Kate on why they were heading for Putney and to try and locate Barbara Hawkes. Alice explained, "Looking at the electoral role this is quite a stable residential area. Many people have lived there for years. I noticed that Barbara Hawkes lived opposite the address we have for both Melissa Smith and

Sylvie Hardcastle on their records. Last year Barbara Hawkes is not on the register but I can't find a death certificate for her so I wondered if she had moved into care, hopefully in the same area."

"That really is a long shot. So, we're hoping that someone will know what has happened to her?"

Alice agreed, "And there were two other residents that were living in that road at the same time as Smith and Hardcastle but both at the far end of the road so they may not have known them or Barbara Hawkes."

Kate looked down at her shoes and smiled gently, remembering Jude and the kiss. Then she brought herself back to the task in hand. "What did you find out about what happened to Sylvie Hardcastle after our victim moved on?"

Alice riffled through her own file and pulled out a sheet, passing it to Kate. Reading it was depressing. It seemed one disaster lead to another, time after time. Hardcastle had several cautions about picking up babies from their prams outside shops and the like. Then in 1977 she had a custodial sentence passed on her for kidnapping a seven month old boy from outside the local post office. It seemed the police knew exactly who had taken him and where to find her and the baby was missing for less than an hour.

Kate was surprised that there had not been a mental health case made for her. On release

Hardcastle then had a number of charges for drug dealing and taking. Finally leading to another prison term. It was not until 2003 that Hardcastle was referred for psychiatric care after another child abduction, this one for more than three days. At that point the trail stopped until a death certificate issued in 2007.

◆ ◆ ◆

Three hours later Kate and Alice turned into Holmbush Road in Putney. It was a leafy, residential road with well cared for homes and gardens. It was easy to find where Smith, aka Grace, and Hardcastle had lived. It was a large Victorian house complete with attic rooms for the servants. It had clearly been divided into flats and it had been in one of these that the two women had lived. Opposite was the house where Barbara Hawkes had lived.

Kate turned in through the gate. Her concern was that with it being a week day they may well not find anyone home. She knocked and they waited. Their luck was in, they could see a shadow moving beyond the glass door. Shortly it was opened by a young woman balancing a toddler on her hip, "Yes, can I help you?"

Kate explained who they were and why they were here. "Do you know where the previous tenant has moved to?"

The woman shook her head. "Sorry, I've no

idea. The house was already empty when we came to look at it the first time." She was beginning to close the door when she pulled it open again, "Hang on, you might want to try Marian at number twenty-five. She seems to be quite friendly with many of the older residents. I know she shops for a couple of them."

"Marian?" Kate queried.

The woman shrugged her shoulders, "Sorry, I've no idea what her last name is." The child on her hip began to wriggle and once again she began to close the door.

Kate said their thanks and turned away. "Okay number twenty-five it is."

The woman at twenty-five, Marian Glancing, was much more forthcoming beginning their interaction with, "Come in and sit. I've got a brew on the go."

Once settled in the back garden under a gazebo, sipping tea, Kate explained why they were there. "Barbara Hawkes, a lovely lady. I used to shop for her when the weather was bad. She had really bad arthritis and although she would insist on going for a walk every day the wet always made it twice as bad and she would relent and stay in."

"Do you know where she has moved to?" Kate asked.

The woman looked surprised, "Of course. I visit her at least once a week. She's gone to Oak Court." Recollecting that Kate and Alice were strangers in town, she elaborated. "Oak Court Residential Home. It's less than a ten minute walk away. I can give you directions."

"How long have you lived here?" Alice asked conversationally.

"Oh only thirty-one years. Babs had lived here since the late sixties. I don't know of anyone else who has lived here as long as she has. It's a nice area and people don't tend to move on."

Having thanked Mrs Glancing for their refreshments and directions, Kate and Alice set off to find Barbara Hawkes at Oak Court. The directions were spot on and ten minutes later Kate was explaining to the manager of the home who they were and why they needed to speak with Barbara Hawkes.

CHAPTER 54

Oak Court was a purpose built residential home. Each resident had their own bed/sitting room with an en-suite and took their meals in a communal area on each floor. Barbara Hawkes had been a tallish woman but arthritis had curled much of her spine, hands and feet. But her eyes were alert and she smiled in pleasure at her visitors.

Once again, Kate explained that they were trying to find out about Sylvie Hardcastle and her baby. "Poor Sylvie, she was never the same after she gave up her baby. Lovely girl, not like the other one, Melissa. She was a hard case that one but Sylvie thought the sun shone out of her backside!"

"Did you know them well, Mrs Hawkes?"

"Call me Babs. I know she's long dead but Mrs Hawkes just reminds me of my mother-in-law. I knew both girls but it was Sylvie I had a soft spot for. I lived opposite their flat. They had one of the attic rooms."

"Having seen the road, didn't other residents mind them having," Kate searched for the right word, "guests in and out."

"You mean the men, don't you? It didn't happen much at the flat. They were high class girls and cars would come and collect them and bring them home. You rarely saw men coming to their address."

"So you knew what they were doing?"

"Yes and I didn't condemn them. Women alone had limited opportunities. You see, when my husband died, pancreatic cancer in 1969, I had to make ends meet."

Seeing the look on Alice's face, she broke off and laughed until she wheezed. "No," she continued, "I didn't go on the game, I did home hairdressing. Clients either came to me or I went to them. Both Sylvie and the other one would have me set and blow dry their hair at least once a week."

"So you knew about their work and knew when Sylvie got pregnant?"

"Yes, poor love. She was so torn up about it but I encouraged her to give him away to the Rogers. They were a lovely couple and desperately wanted a child. They would have given him a much better life than she could. But it seemed to break her. That and the other one moving on."

"Did you know she sold the baby?" Kate asked.

Babs' eyes opened in horror and then tears formed and fell. Sylvie wouldn't have sold her baby." She closed her eyes for a few seconds and then opened them, speaking vehemently. "Now I understand why Melissa offered to do all the toing and froing between Sylvie and the Rogers.

I thought at the time it showed a surprising sensitivity on her part but now it makes sense. She sold that baby? She took money for him?"

"As far as we understand it, yes."

"Well, Sylvie didn't see a great deal of it. She was just chuffed that Melissa had left her a little extra. Conniving little bitch. I never did like her. Pah!" Babs almost spat, so disgusted was she.

"Do you know where the Rogers are now?"

Babs shook her head. "They thought it would be too much for Sylvie to see her child being brought up by them so once the baby was theirs they moved away. Milton Keynes, I think."

"Do you know their names?" Alice asked with pencil and notebook ready.

"She was Shirley. I knew her quite well as I did her hair every week, too. I know that baby would have been loved and cared for by her. His name, the husband, I mean, now he was," a pause as she searched her memory banks. "I think he was Keith. Keith Rogers. Yes, I think that's right."

"Do you know what name they gave the child? A boy, you said?"

"Yes, a little boy. I had a cuddle with him when he was less than a day old. I'm not sure I know the name they gave him." She thought for a while and then shook her head again.

Further discussion elicited no more useful information and Kate thanked Barbara Hawkes for her time.

"It's been lovely having visitors and

remembering the old days. I won't say 'good old days' because a lot of hurt happened in the past but I do miss the likes of Sylvie."

Her eyes were already beginning to close as Kate and Alice collected their things and made to leave. Milton Keynes, Kate thought. Okay, that's where they were off to.

CHAPTER 55

Whilst Alice used her phone to work out their best route to Milton Keynes, Kate contacted Colm. "Can you do some tracking down for me? Shirley and Keith Rogers moved from Putney to Milton Keynes in 1971. Can you see if you can get a current address? They'd be about mid sixties to mid-seventies I should imagine."

"No probs, boss. Len is having no joy on car hire, so far," Colm's voice dropped, "not a happy bunny!"

Kate smiled. "I know. The women are off having a jolly and the men are holding the fort doing all the boring stuff!"

Colm snorted. "You must be a mind reader."

"Email me whatever you can find on the Rogers, please."

Alice looked up from her phone. "It's going to be a couple of hours to get to Milton Keynes."

Kate sighed, "I hope you haven't got plans for this evening," as she thought of her previous evening. "Let's head towards the station and find somewhere to get something to eat and drink. I don't want to head for Milton Keynes and then find the Rogers have moved back into London."

They soon found an Italian café and decided to sit outside. The traffic was preferable to the humidity inside the place. Having ordered, they reviewed their morning.

"I know we shouldn't judge but I don't like the sound of our victim very much," said Alice pulling a grimace. "She seems to have spent her whole life using people and as for selling the baby…" She frowned, before continuing, "Bad enough to sell it in the first place but to sell it and not give the money to the mother, that's callous."

Kate had to agree. It wasn't down to them to judge their victim – they were here to solve a crime; regardless of the crimes the victim had committed. "I agree, but we have to remember that her death was a crime and although we may find mitigating circumstances, that's not down to us. We apprehend the murderer and the justice system metes out the punishment."

"I know, but… I don't know. It's just somehow harder when you don't actually like what you're finding out about someone."

Their food and drink arrived. "You have to know about the life of the victim to track down why someone would want them dead but you don't have to like them. Actually sometimes it helps if you don't like them. The killer cases are those where you get involved with the victim. Those are the hardest to work."

Alice nodded as she bit into her panini. At the same moment Kate's email alert sounded. She checked it and looked up. "Milton Keynes it is. It seems Keith Rogers died in 1999 so it's just Shirley we'll see. Colm says according to the electoral register she's living alone. I wonder where the son is living."

CHAPTER 56

As Colm sent off the email to Kate, Len called out, "We might have something here." Colm walked across and leant over Len's shoulder as Len continued, "A Mr Brian Collins reported a small van blocking the lane that runs along the back of our victim's house during the week leading up to her murder. He made his complaint on the Saturday after she disappeared."

Any details, like a reg?" Colm asked hopefully.

Len clicked through several screens. "No, apparently the third time he saw it, which was when he decided to complain, it was night."

"Well, it's got to be worth a follow up, don't you think?"

Len passed Colm a contact number so he could phone Mr Collins. A few minutes later after a brief telephone conversation Colm asked Len, "Do you fancy stretching your legs and joining me on this interview?"

Len leapt up, picked his uniform jacket from the back of his chair and followed Colm from the office.

Hawthorne Road ran at right angles to their victim's road and number 6 was at the edge of the back lane. Colm knocked sharply and waited a few seconds. When the door opened, a tall man with damp hair stood before them. He was in his shirt sleeves, "DC Hunter?"

Colm produced his warrant card and introduced PC Goodfellow.

"Come on in then. You'll have to excuse me but I need to sort meself out some breakfast."

Colm peered at his watch, it was after one in the afternoon.

Clearly, Colm had not been discreet enough, "I'm on night shifts this week, ten til six so I've just got up and it's breakfast time."

Colm felt guilty, "I'm sorry, did I wake you?"

"Nah. I'm normally on the move about one." He gestured to a small table with two chairs tucked in. There was barely room for all three men in the kitchen. "If you two sit there, I'll work round you."

Colm felt overly large sat at the table and he saw that Len felt equally cramped. He hit his elbow on the wall as he tried to retrieve his notebook. "I know it's a long time ago but do you remember in August 2015 you contacted us to complain about a van blocking the back lane?"

"Bloomin' heck. That's going back. But yes, I remember. I use that lane as a cut through on my way to work on the bike. With that van there I had to squeeze past pushing the bike in front. Bloomin' nuisance!"

"How many times did you see it in the lane?"

"Three times in one week. The first two times I thought someone must be having stuff delivered and it was awkward but the third time it was at night and I ended up tearing my trousers. I was so mad it kept me going until the next day when I phoned the station."

"How far along the lane was it parked?"

Collins stopped cutting the loaf on the bread board and waved the knife in his hand. He directed it through the window to the lane running down the side. There's not many who use their back gates but the van was parked outside one where you could see from the wear on the grass that someone was using it. About," he paused for thought, "five, maybe six houses along."

"Did you get the registration number?" Colm held his breath and sighed with disappointment as Collins explained that it had been too dark to see on the third time when he decided to report it.

"Did the van have any sort of logo or name on it?"

Collins shook his head. With his back to them as he fried himself egg and bacon, he moved with practiced ease around the kitchen's small space. "But I did see it in town about a week later and took a photo." Collins was grinning as he turned back to face them. "I'd just got a new smartphone and was trying out the camera. I saw the van and snapped it."

"How did you know it was the same van if it didn't have any identifying features?" queried

Colm.

"It didn't have any logo and such but it did have the back doors tied up with bright orange nylon rope. It looked like someone had tried to break in and bust the lock and this was the only way to keep the doors shut."

Colm still wasn't ready to celebrate. This was three years ago. Did Collins even have the same phone? "My son downloaded all my pics onto the computer." Collins disappeared and returned with a laptop in hand. "Look, you go through it on here," he placed it on the only spare surface on the work top, "and let me sit and eat."

Colm jumped up and squeezed himself past Collins. The laptop wasn't password protected and Colm was soon looking at a series of photos and there it was. In fact there they were. Two photos of a small white van, the registration plate clearly visible, along with the rope tying the back doors together. Colm noted the details down.

"Mr Collins, can you be sure what night it was the van was blocking the lane?"

Looking thoughtful with a fork of bacon and toast half way to his mouth, Collins then lowered it. "I know it was a Friday. Fridays are our change over day for shifts. So I'd moved from two to ten on Wednesday night, Thursday off and new shift, ten to six, on the Friday. God knows what the date was but it was the night before I made the complaint."

"Thank you Mr Collins. You have been very helpful. We'll leave you to finish your breakfast in peace."

Collins went to rise but Colm put a hand on his shoulder, "Don't worry, we'll see ourselves out."

CHAPTER 57

As soon as they left the house, Len was on the radio to get the registered keeper's details from the station. Colm strode to the lane and walked up it. He could see how a vehicle, no matter how small, would cause a blockage. The lane was very narrow and the vegetation had spread from the sides, making the space even smaller. Colm soon saw what Collins had meant about not many back gates being in use. Most were clogged with weeds but one wasn't and when Colm stepped through and peered round the bushes he saw it was, indeed their victim's garden.

Turning back, Colm saw Len waiting for him at the mouth to the lane. As he approached, Len said, "Got the keeper. It belongs to Duckets & Sons, the builders merchants on the Shearing Road."

"Right, let's go."

The journey was a quick one and both men were buoyant with expectation. Had they finally got the lead they needed? The builder's yard was busy with flatbed trucks and the inevitable white vans. Colm sneaked their car into a space by the fence and made their way inside the building. It was a massive aluminium construction with floor to ceiling shelving holding everything a builder may need in the pursuit of his work. And it was busy.

At one end there was a counter that ran the length of the building and several men in brown warehouse coats were serving along the entire length. Colm espied an older man and made a guess that he would be the manager, if not the Mr Duckets who owned the place. Hovering behind the man being served, Colm held up his warrant card until the older man acknowledged he had seen it and then he and Len stepped to one side.

A good ten minutes later, the older man approached them with hand outstretched. "Sorry about that. It's a bit manic at the moment. How can I help you?" His hair was thick and shot through with grey. Colm guessed that it had once been black and that, along with his olive complexion, wondered what name had been anglicised to achieve Duckets.

"Mr Duckets?" Colm queried.

"Which one? I'm Joseph Duckets, original Duckets owner. Then there is my son, Joe and my grandson Joey."

"You, thank you." The air was riven by the crash of metal on metal. It didn't seem to perturb Mr Duckets but it did make conversation difficult. "Could we go somewhere quieter, please?"

Mr Duckets walked to one end of the counter and opened a door into a back office. Len and Colm tracked his movements and then moved forward as Duckets lifted a section of the counter top. "Come through this way."

With the door shut, the noise diminished to a background growl. "Now, what is it you want?" Duckets asked as he stepped behind a desk and sat whilst indicating two plastic chairs on one side of the office.

Colm and Len pulled them across to the desk and Colm began, "Do you own a white van, with this reg number?" Colm handed across a slip of paper with the details on.

Duckets ran a hand through his hair, "Don't tell me one of those silly buggers has been speeding?"

"So, you do own it?"

Duckets sighed, "Yes. When was it? I can check their worksheets and find out who was driving."

"Do your worksheets go back to August 2015?"

Duckets had been in mid-rise from his seat and then sat back down heavily. "2015? Blimey I didn't think they did cold cases for driving tickets."

Colm smiled. "No, not a driving ticket. We're following up on some information that may help us with a case we're working on."

Duckets rose again. "Okay. Hang on a sec, I'll see if Jenny can track them down."

He left them and disappeared through the second door in the office. Colm looked around. The office was purely functional. Desk, chairs, a computer and telephone were its only furniture. Duckets returned with a sheaf of papers in his hands, already flicking through them. Rather than sitting down he went to the first door and called through. "Joey, in here on the double." He closed the door and returned to his seat.

"Joey, my grandson was doing most of the deliveries that summer. He was waiting for his exam results and whether he was going on to university." Duckets continued to shift through the papers. "Do you have a specific date in mind?"

Colm checked his notes. If August 15 was the Friday and Collins claimed that the van had blocked the lane twice in the previous week, he needed to see the week beginning August 11. He told Duckets this who then resumed his flicking through.

"Got it."

He looked intently at the sheet and then scratched his head. He looked up, "According to the worksheets it should have been Joey but his name's been crossed through. I don't know who was driving."

Colm's heart sank. To be so close! At that point Joey Duckets entered. Colm thought he could see his grandfather in this young man's face and there was certainly black hair. "Okay Gramps? What do you need?"

Duckets senior passed across the worksheet for the week of August 11, 2015. "Do you remember why you didn't do the driving that week?"

Duckets junior scratched his head, a mirror gesture of his grandfather and then a slow smile spread across his face. "Yeh, of course. Don't you remember Gramps? I broke my leg moving those scaffolding poles."

Another head scratch, "Ah, yes. So, who did the driving for the rest of that summer?"

"Will Miller! He offered and asked to be paid in kind." At this point Duckets junior turned to Colm and Len. "Will's been renovating a cottage and was always in and out. You remember, Gramps."

"So, would Will Miller have had sole use of the van for the week in question?" Colm wanted a definitive answer.

"Yes. He asked if he could use it for shifting stuff from his cottage to the dump and taking stuff from here. He did the driving for about two weeks. By then hopalong here could help out the front and one of the other blokes could do the driving."

"What about in the evenings?"

"I told him to take it home. We'd had a break-in in the yard and they'd bust the lock of that van. I think they were looking for tools. So it seemed to me it would be as safe at his place as in the yard," Duckets senior explained.

"Thank you sir. Could you and your grandson attend the station at your own convenience at some point this week to make a formal statement?"

"A formal statement!" Joey was both surprised and, Colm guessed, excited. "Are we helping with a real case?"

"Yes sir." Colm rose and thanked them both before he and Len left through the frenetic customers massed in the warehouse.

CHAPTER 58

The journey to Milton Keynes was slow and hot. Finally, two and a bit hours later Kate and Alice stood outside Milton Keynes central. Peeling her shirt off her back, Kate said, "I don't care how much it costs, we're getting a taxi from here."

Alice smiled her approval. The taxi took turning after turning as they left the station and Kate was glad of her decision. She'd never been to Milton Keynes and admired the wide boulevards of the town centre but lost track of where they were or even which direction they were going in.

Douglas Place was typical of the architecture of the '60s and '70s. Shirley Rogers lived in a maisonette in a block of four. The front of the building was paved and given over to parking. Mrs Rogers lived in one of the ground floor sections. Kate knocked and had her warrant card ready in her hand.

The door opened and although Kate knew Shirley Rogers must be in her seventies the woman who stood before them looked good for her age.

"Mrs Shirley Rogers?" Kate held up her card and knew that Alice was mirroring her action behind her.

The woman put her hand to her mouth and her face lost all colour, "Not Tom. Don't tell me something has happened to Tom?"

Kate hastened to reassure her. "As far as we know Tom is fine, Mrs Rogers, but we would like to ask you a few questions about him."

The woman put a steadying hand to the door frame, "Sorry. You see two police officers at your door and you think the worst." The colour had begun to return to her face, although she still looked pale.

"May we come in?"

"Of course. Sorry. Come in." She stepped back and held the door wide.

Kate and Alice stood in a small vestibule. Shirley Rogers pointed through the door and they entered a compact front room. It was adequate and tidy. The furniture would once have been top of the range but now showed a gentile shabbiness. "You take the sofa," Mrs Rogers directed as she sat in the chair showing the most wear. "Now what is it you want with Tom?"

Kate had thought hard about how to approach this interview. She didn't want to alarm Shirley Rogers and she didn't want her to clam up about anything to do with Tom or the adoption. "We're aware that you undertook a private adoption for Tom from Sylvie Hardcastle."

Rogers sat perfectly still, only the white of her knuckles holding the end of the chair arms indicated her inner stress. "And I wondered if he was aware of his adoption?"

Her voice shaking slightly, she replied, "We did nothing wrong."

Kate nodded her agreement. She had checked and private adoptions didn't become illegal until 1983, although the manner of this one was somewhat unorthodox.

Encouraged, Mrs Rogers continued, "She was a lovely woman, Sylvie, but there was no way she could have coped with a baby on her own. She could barely manage looking after herself. We could offer Tom so much more."

"When did you tell Tom about his birth mother?"

"When he turned eighteen. Sylvie came to see me a few weeks before Tom was born and gave me a letter. She asked that I give it to Tom when he was eighteen. Sylvie promised that there was nothing horrible in it, just an explanation of why she couldn't keep him."

"Did you read the letter?"

"No. I trusted Sylvie when she said the type of letter it was." Her tone changed, "Why are you asking these questions. Has Tom done something wrong?"

"As far as we are aware, Tom has done nothing wrong but his name has come up in connection with a case we are working on, so we need to rule him out of our investigations."

"What case?"

"I'm not at liberty to say but please believe

me when I say we are looking to dismiss Tom from our enquiries."

The woman relaxed a little but Kate wasn't convinced that she was happy with the answer. She continued, "How did Tom take it? The letter?"

"Remarkably well. He was a bit confused because he had a proper birth certificate. Keith and I had registered him as ours." She looked a little bashful, "but he said the letter didn't change anything."

"Did you also tell him about the exchange of money?"

"I did," she said firmly, "I wanted him to understand that we were trying to do the best for both him and his mother."

"Did he want to track his birth mother down?"

Rogers shook her head. "Not then, no, but after his father, Keith, died, he did begin a family search. It was very difficult for him because it had been a private adoption so there wasn't a paper trail."

"Did he find his birth mother?"

Rogers shook her head. "I don't think so. He's never mentioned it to me."

"Where is Tom now? I gather he doesn't live with you?"

"Good grief, no! He's a grown man. He has his own life to lead. He's in Taunton at the moment working for a biotechnical company."

"What does he do?" Alice asked.

"I don't really understand it but it's something to do with working out computer programmes to predict outcomes and then investigating when things don't do as predicted," she paused and reviewed what she'd said, "I think!"

"Does he visit home often?"

"He's not great at getting home but we email one another every week or so. He's really enjoying his work and making a life for himself. I just wish he'd find a nice girl and really settle down. I worry that he'll be on his own when I'm gone."

"Do you have an address for him?" Alice asked, pen poised.

Rogers looked uncomfortable and shook her head. "He says he'll let me know once he's settled somewhere. At the moment he's just doing short-term lets." As though unsure whether this sounded good enough, she continued, "I think he'd like to buy somewhere but you know what the housing market is like for first time buyers."

"What about a telephone number?" Alice persisted.

Rogers brightened, "Oh yes. I have that." She reached for the phone in its cradle on the table at the side of her chair. She pressed a button, looked up and checked that Alice was ready and read out the number. "He's not allowed to have his mobile on in work and he says there are some black spots signal wise, so quite often I have to leave a message and wait for him to get back to me."

"Thank you Mrs Rogers, you have been very helpful."

"So can you rule Tom out of your case?"

Kate fudged her answer, "We'd like to confirm a few details with Tom himself first."

As they were leaving, Alice asked, "Do you know the name of Tom's firm?"

"Biotech Solutions," Rogers replied promptly. "I had a look at their website. Very impressive. Not that I understood a word of it really," she finished self-deprecatingly.

CHAPTER 59

The taxi driver that Kate had had the forethought to ask to wait, was stood against his taxi drinking and wetting a handkerchief from a bottle of water. He then wiped the back of his neck and forehead. Seeing Kate and Alice exiting the house, he screwed tight the bottle and slipped back into his driver's seat. Even with all the windows open, the inside of the car was akin to a sauna and Kate was grateful as they got moving and a slight breeze made its way inside.

Aware of the driver's presence, the two women kept their conversation light and inconsequential. At the railway station Alice worked out their best route home while Kate asked for a receipt from the driver. It was a sign of the times, she mused, that taxi drivers now had card machines. As the taxi drove away, Alice indicated her mobile screen, "It's back into London, Euston station and then across to Paddington. We've missed those that avoid London and go via Birmingham. It looks like we're not going to be home before about eight-thirty."

"We'll pick up a drink and snacks here and something more substantial at Paddington, if we have enough time."

"Not sure we've got time for drinks here. In

fact I think we've only got five minutes." With that the pair briskly walked into the station and sought their platform. Platform 2. Damn. Up and over the bridge. Already, the announcer was giving the stations of the train now arriving at that platform. They broke into a trot and lumbered down the stairs just as the train drew to a halt. A little breathless, they clambered aboard and found seats.

"Phew! I hope they have a trolley service," Kate said, aware of how dry her throat felt.

Alice nodded her agreement and then, once the train was underway, spoke quietly to Kate, "Do you think Tom Rogers has anything to do with our case? Really?"

Kate ran her fingers through her damp hair, a sure sign of frustration. "I honestly don't know. I'd wondered if Tom was behind the letters Grace received in the years before her death. But Mrs Rogers doesn't seem to think that he found anything when he went looking."

"Unless he didn't want to tell her. You know, feeling a bit guilty talking to his real mother about tracking down his birth one."

Kate rubbed her nose. "You could be right. We still don't know enough about him. I just want a few more details before we rule him out."

Kate's phone rang, it was Colm. Kate listened intently and Alice watched her face trying to work out what was being said. A broad grin spread across Kate's face and her next words confirmed that Colm must have found out something, "I want as deep a search as possible about Will Miller, but don't alert him to our interest. Well done you two. We'll all debrief in the morning. Alice and I are not going to be back before about nine tonight. Okay?"

Finishing the call, Kate updated Alice on Colm and Len's findings. "So it could be Will Miller is our murderer."

Alice's face fell. "So everything we've done today is worthless for the case?"

"Not necessarily. We have to follow all the threads. Colm and Len may have tugged on a really important one but we don't have all the info we need yet."

Alice brightened, "Shall I research Tom Rogers' firm? Biotech Solutions, wasn't it?"

"Yes, in Taunton, not a million miles from us. So he's still a contender."

Kate began to quietly record her impressions and key points from their interview with Shirley Rogers and Alice began to search for her son's firm. Each was intent on their task until the welcome rattle of the refreshment trolley caught their attention. A hot and a cold drink each and a stack of snacks. Later, their mutual silence was broken by a whispered, "Yes!" from Alice.

Kate looked up. Alice was grinning from ear to ear. "Guess what one of the projects Biotech Solutions is involved in with a German firm."

Kate shook her head.

"Only the use of mycelium mats to use in coffins to aid decomposition!"

Kate's eyes widened, "You are kidding? So now we have two possible candidates. One had motive but what about the means? The other had the means but what is his motive?"

"We're getting there aren't we, boss?"

Kate nodded, "I think we are."

CHAPTER 60

Wednesday morning, Kate sprung out of bed. They were almost there. She could feel it in her bones. The trouble was that if they were successful today she would be spending her evening putting together a report for the CPS and Jude had texted to suggest a meal one evening soon. Should she warn her it wouldn't be as soon as they wished? In the end she sent a quick text, "Hi Jude, just to warn you my case may come to a head today. Once it is closed, perhaps we can get together again?"

Despite the early hour, there was an almost immediate response, "Hope you are successful. Maybe a celebratory meal later in the week? Jx." She must be on an early shift, Kate surmised.

The response made Kate feel light-hearted. Perhaps there was a future in her romantic life.

On the way into the office, Kate picked up coffees and a box of Danish. Good will and sugar might oil the old brain cells, she thought. Whilst awaiting the arrival of the others, she rearranged the murder board, leaving space to create two columns; one labelled Tom Rogers and the other Will Miller.

The others arrived almost simultaneously and Kate told them to collect food and drink and gather by the board. Once everyone was settled, she began and gave a summary of what she and Alice had discovered the day before. She concluded with, "Tom Rogers remains a person of interest because," and she began to make notes on the board, "if he found out about his mother not getting the money and the state she was in later, that would give him motive."

"And his firm is involved with mycelium mats for aiding decomposition," Alice added.

Kate wrote the point on the board but then Colm played Devil's advocate, "But how did he know about the field and the trees? Surely that's got to be a local?"

Kate nodded, "I agree. Colm give us a quick rundown of your success yesterday."

Colm took the stage and gave a brief overview before Kate took over again and wrote under Will Miller's name, "Access to a vehicle and one spotted the night of the murder." Turning to the room, Kate then asked, "But what's his motive?"

"Miller and Rogers working together?" Len suggested.

Kate wrote the idea on the board but bracketed it with large question marks. No-one else had anything else to offer, "Okay. May I suggest that we stay in yesterday's teams and that Colm, you and Len do research on Will Miller. Everything you can possibly find. Alice and I will do the same for Tom Rogers. Agreed?"

Nods from all. Kate put the board pen back on its base and concluded, "We'll break for lunch at twelve-thirty and feedback what we've found."

Everyone broke away to their desks and

within minutes all that was heard was the click of the computer keyboards. "Alice, I'm going to call Biotech Solutions and see if Tom Rogers is available for a chat later today."

Before reaching for her desk phone Kate looked at the business' web page. Although there were several pictures and biographies on their various project pages, Tom Rogers was not amongst them. Using the displayed number, Kate phoned.

At the third ring the phone was answered where Kate introduced herself and asked to be put through to Tom Rogers. The receptionist replied, "One moment please," and the inevitable piped music began. Only a short time later the voice came back on line, "I'm sorry but we do not have a Tom Rogers working at this office."

Thinking quickly, Kate asked for the HR Manager. Once again piped music and then a cheerful voice came on, "Mark Masefield, HR. How may I help you?"

Kate introduced herself again and asked if they had any record for Tom Rogers. Had he ever worked for them? Was he in another branch?"

"I doubt if he's in another branch as they are all overseas, but let me just check through the records. Kate could hear the click of a mouse and the quiet breathing of Mr Masefield and then, "Ah, here we go. Tom Rogers. He did work for us but left in 2010. Let me check the details." Another quiet space and then, "Apparently, he worked in our biochemical wing and he asked for a six month sabbatical, which we couldn't accommodate."

"Did he explain why he wanted this sabbatical?"

"Let me see... No. Just personal reasons. Shortly after that he resigned."

"Do you have any contact details for him?"

"I have a mobile but no forwarding address as such. It's a PO Box in Taunton." He gave Kate the number, which was the same as the one Shirley Rogers had provided. They'd already tried that and had got the answerphone. At the moment Kate did not want to leave a message. Thanking Mr Masefield for his time and help, Kate replaced her receiver. She then turned to her computer. This was good old fashioned policing. Research and more research. She set to. Alice was doing the historical research and Kate had opted for present day. So first things first, find your Tom Rogers!

CHAPTER 61

Kate glanced at her watch, not quite twelve. The last few hours had been one of relentless frustration. Wherever Tom Rogers was at the moment he was keeping a very low profile. She couldn't find a trace of him. Looking at her team she could tell from their body language that none of them had experienced a eureka moment.

"Okay team. I know it's not twelve but unless you're hot on a trail, shall we break for lunch and debrief?"

Groans and stretches greeted her question and all three swivelled round to face her. Colm added a giant yawn to his actions and Alice rubbed her eyes. Taking this as agreement, Kate continued, "Right we'll go and get lunch but bring it back here so we can update one another."

Kate thought she heard Len moan, "Precious little from me." She was afraid that they were all on a losing streak. How could they be so close but not be able to move forward?

It was a dispirited team that reformed around the table with their lunches. Kate led the discussion through mouthfuls of her sandwich. "Rogers no longer works for Biotech Solutions and I can't find any trace of him from 2010 apart from the fact that his PO Box is still active in Taunton. Alice, can you add to that?"

"Not after 2010, no. He was one of the first to have a Facebook account in 2005 but he wasn't very active on it and nothing has been posted since those early days. No other social media activity that I can find. I know what school he went to, what grades he got at GCSE and what uni he went to but nothing after 2010. It's like he's fallen off the face of the earth!"

"Unless he's changed his name," Len offered.

A thought was beginning to coalesce in Kate's mind. "Colm? Len? What have you got on Will Miller?"

Colm swallowed his mouthful and cleared his throat. "He has an account in Eashire Providential and paid cash for his cottage. Not, however, the five thousand he said but twenty-five thousand. He had a healthy amount in 2010, when he opened the account and it has diminished bit by bit, I assume as he has bought materials for his renovation. Many of the amounts are to Duckets & Sons."

Colm looked across to Len, who took up the report, "He also has no social media presence and I can't find any history of him before 2010."

"What, nothing at all? Not even a birth certificate?"

"Nope, not a thing."

"So, has he changed his name as well?" Alice asked.

Kate's thoughts were in order, "What if Tom Rogers and Will Miller are one and the same?"

Everybody stopped their lunch and looked at Kate. "It would make sense," Kate continued, enlarging on her idea, "it would account for why we can't find anything about Tom Rogers after 2010 and Will Miller before that time, wouldn't it?"

Colm's chewing slowed and then his head began an even slower nod, "You might have a point there, boss."

"It would then give us means and motive," Alice agreed.

"Right, Alice, have you finished lunch?"

"Yes, boss," replied Alice as she threw the last mouthful in the bin.

"Give Mrs Rogers a ring and ask if she has a recent photo of her son. She seemed computer literate, talking about looking on the website at Tom's place of work, hopefully she can scan and send."

"Len, what about you? Finished?"

Len guzzled the last of his fizzy drink, burped behind his hand and nodded.

"Access deed poll records and see if we can track a name change. We maybe lucky and he's done it officially."

"Colm, you and I are going to re-read the letters. There must be something in them that we can tie to one or both of these two men."

Less than ten minutes later, "I've got it!" Kate said, as she put down the page she was reading. "Colm, when we interviewed Will Miller, what did he say about how he contacted our victim?"

Colm scratched his head and looked through his notes. Having found the right page, he read out, "He sent a letter telling her that he would be her gardener."

"No, he didn't!" Kate said and Colm looked surprised, "He said he sent her a missive. What does our letter writer call these notes?"

Colm re-read the one in front of him and smiled, "His missives. Oh, well done, boss. I never noticed."

"Not so well done," Kate said ruefully. "It's been bugging me since we interviewed him and it's only just come to the forefront."

Their discussion was interrupted by Alice, "Boss, Mrs Rogers had a photo on her computer, it's her screensaver, apparently."

Colm and Kate hurried across to Alice's desk. Staring at them was Will Miller. Younger, perhaps less fit, but most definitely Will Miller. "Hello Tom Rogers, aka Will Miller," Kate said quietly.

Len called across, "Good you can confirm with the photo because these records are not showing an official change of name."

"Well done everyone. Colm, you and I have a visit to make."

"Do you want to ring first?"

"No, let's not alert him. We'll try Grace's house first and then his home. Have you got his address?"

"Yes," Colm waved his notebook.
"Let's go and make an arrest."

CHAPTER 62

As Colm followed Kate out of the station he asked, "Why aren't we just bringing him in for questioning, boss?"

"I want to tie up the forensics evidence from the letters, scant as it is. Soil, soot and mushrooms."

"You think the letter writer is Rogers/Miller?"

"Yes. Do you remember when we went to check out whether the garden at our victim's house had a back entrance? Miller was sketching a patio design…"

"In a spiral bound notebook!" Colm finished for her. "But what about the soot?"

"My guess is that he's got an open fire in the cottage or he's been cleaning out the chimneys."

"And the mushrooms?"

"There I'm not so sure. His biotech firm was certainly involved in research into their use but where would he grow what he needed?"

"And it would need to be a large amount if Gus thinks the body was wrapped or covered with it."

"Precisely. So, we still have evidence and questions. Let's see if we can answer them."

Colm drove and took Kate round to the back lane entrance. He explained what Mr Collins had seen and when. Kate could see quite clearly that their victim's garden entrance was the only one that showed regular use. Walking along the lane she could see that any vehicle parked there would be out of view of the houses the lane backed onto because of the height of the trees and bushes. Only if, like Mr Collins, you were using the lane as a cut through would you know about any van left here.

While Kate examined the lane, Colm went through to the garden of their victim's house. A few minutes later he reappeared and shook his head. "The shed is padlocked and there's no sign of any garden activity underway."

"Right. His home address it is."

The renovated cottage was easy to find. It was the only building of any age in the short road. "You have to admire his drive. Did you see the photo he showed us on his mobile? This place was derelict. Now it looks great."

Kate looked the building over as she climbed out of the car. She could see that the roof was new but that Miller had attempted to blend in old and new tiles. The brick walls had been repointed and new guttering fringed the roof.

"Those windows were practically falling out," said Colm, pointing to the windows at the front. Kate was no expert but she thought it looked as if Miller had maintained the old glass. It rippled more than new glass.

As they made their way towards the cottage

door, Kate said quietly, "Colm I want you to be his best buddy. Marvel at his work, you know, get him on board. He might even offer you a tour."

Before Kate raised her hand to knock, the door opened and Miller stood in the doorway smiling his welcome, "I don't get many visitors to this place. Come on in."

Miller was casually dressed in jeans and a T-shirt, clearly not the ones he used for gardening. Leaving the door open, he stepped back into the gloom of the cottage. Kate and Colm followed into the kitchen area.

"You're lucky to find me in, I was planning to join the Eashire Ramblers this afternoon."

A hand-built kitchen surrounded a range cooker at one side of the room with a scrubbed wooden table. Closer to the chimney there were comfortable worn wing back chairs.

"Are you a regular member?" Kate asked as she looked around the space.

Miller turned and pointed to a couple of chairs and went and dragged a three-legged stool from the kitchen area. "Not regular but over the years I've plodded a few miles with them." He smiled, settled himself and waited expectantly.

Kate made herself comfortable. She was surprised to see a packet of cigarettes and a gold lighter on the fire mantel. Fit, healthy, outdoors man. She would not have placed Miller as a smoker. She brought her mind back to the task in hand. They had a murderer to confront.

CHAPTER 63

Kate leant back in her chair and allowed Colm to take the lead. He dutifully began to gush. "It's amazing what you have done with this place. I couldn't believe it was the same cottage you showed me in the photo!"

Will Miller smiled. His eyes twinkled and the edges crinkled in his delight at Colm's praise. "It's taken long enough but I am just about finished. I might add a few shelves in here and one of the bedrooms but really that's just cosmetics."

"Well, I take my hat off to you. I wouldn't know where to start, even with the internet. God! You must have spent a fortune on building materials. Who did you use, Duckets? I go there, they're really helpful."

Miller nodded. "Yes, I'm pretty much on first name terms with the blokes in there."

"Didn't you say last time we spoke that you'd just done the last job in here?"

"Yes. I tanked the cellar."

Colm shook his head, "Sorry, you're talking to a complete novice, what does that mean?"

Miller laughed, good naturedly, "The cellar was really damp so I've lined it with a waterproof membrane. It seems to have done the trick but I won't know for sure until we've had the winter rains."

Colm shook his head as though in wonder and then pretended that he had caught Kate's eye, "Sorry boss."

Miller turned to Kate and smiled, "Yes, I'm sure you didn't come here to admire my building skills."

Kate was now sure Miller/Rogers was their man. The dampness of the cellar would have been ideal for growing the mycelium. Now, she needed to ease out a confession.

"We're just following up on some questions," Kate began. "When someone is involved in a case, even on the periphery, we like to research their background. Just to be clear that we know who we're dealing with."

Miller nodded slowly. The twinkle in his eye had died and Kate sensed the tension begin to grow, despite his attempt to appear at ease. She continued, "And we have a problem, Mr Miller. You see we can't find out anything about you before 2010. Now why would that be?"

Miller shrugged and a perplexed look rode across his face. "I don't know why not. Though I'm not into social media and online stuff."

"But we can't even find a National Insurance number for you," Kate said sounding, she hoped, baffled, rather than accusatory. "I am assuming that your employment with Josephine Grace was official? Not cash in hand?"

Colm added, "We know you have a bank account here in Eashire into which your wages from Ms Grace are paid but no accounts before 2010."

"It's as if you appeared amongst us fully grown in 2010!" Kate finished. She watched Miller carefully. Was he going to try and blag his way out of this or come clean about his true identity?

Miller took a deep breath and rested his hands on his thighs. "I'm sorry, I should have told you before but I wanted to leave my old life behind me. I changed my name in 2010."

Kate feigned surprise and then smiled, "That would explain a lot. What was your name prior to 2010, please?" Kate noted that Colm had his pen poised.

It was with some reluctance that Miller answered, "Tom Rogers."

Was he hoping that they hadn't made the connection to the Rogers and Sylvie Hardcastle."

"So, Mr Rogers..."

Rogers held up his hand, "I would like you to use my current name, Will Miller. I haven't changed it by deed poll yet, but I will."

"Certainly, Mr Miller. Could you explain why you changed your name in 2010?"

"Is that really necessary? I did and I have given you my former name."

"It is necessary Mr Miller, for our enquiries. If it turns out to be unimportant then we will proceed no further along this track."

Miller sighed heavily and rearranged his

position on the stool. He crossed his arms but clearly felt uncomfortable and returned his hands to his thighs. "I had a very good childhood but when I was eighteen my parents told me I had been adopted and gave me a letter from my birth mother." He stopped and glanced around the room before continuing, "It was a nice letter. My birth mother explained that she hadn't been in a position to look after me properly and that she knew the Rogers would give me a good life, and they had. At first the letter didn't make any difference but later, after my father, my adoptive father, died, I had a desire to try and track my birth mother down."

"What did your adoptive mother think about that? It must have been hard for her."

Miller looked thoughtful, "Yes it must have been but she was very supportive. Well, to cut a long story short I did find my birth mother. She wasn't very well but we did get to chat and she explained that if she had kept me she would have named me Will, after her grandfather, Will Miller, so I decided to take on a new name."

"How does Mrs Rogers feel about that?" Colm asked.

Miller hung his head, "I haven't told her. We keep in touch via email or phone messages but I don't get home very often. I think it would sound ungrateful if I told her I had changed my name. It's why I haven't done the deed poll bit yet."

"So, once you had talked with Sylvie

Hardcastle, is that when you decided to write to Josephine Grace?"

Miller's head shot round to stare at Kate and his eyes widened.

CHAPTER 64

The kitchen was silent and Kate heard from somewhere in the cottage the loud tick of a clock. Miller took a few moments to collect himself.

"I wondered if she'd kept them."

"Why did you write them?"

Miller looked surprised, "You've read them. Don't you think she needed to be called to account?"

"How did you know what she was up to?"

Miller smiled, "As I said, I did find my birth mother, Sylvie, and she recognised me. Knew I was her son. But she was in a poor state of health, both physical and mental. She never could come to terms with getting rid of me. It virtually broke her. God knows what would have happened if she found out about the money." He began to frown. "I only had a little over eighteen months with her but she was a sweet person and it tore me up to see her so fragile. It made me angry with Sally Price."

He stared vacantly, not seeing either Kate or Colm, and then continued, "My birth mother left me everything when she died. Not that there was much in material terms but her main possessions were her diaries. She'd kept a diary since she was eleven years old. It was so sad reading all her dreams and plans for the future and knowing what happened to her later." Tears filled his eyes but did not shed.

He shook himself and adjusted his position on the stool. "I used the diaries to piece together hers and Sally Price's life. I knew about the money the Rogers had paid and how my mother saw precious little of it. How Josey," the smile was now a sneer, "used my mother. I'm sure she never gave Sylvie another thought once she had the money." For years I thought about what she had done and how I could make her feel guilty and then one evening fate stepped in."

He looked across to Kate, "Have your enquiries come across Craig Masters?"

Kate nodded.

"So you know what Price was trying to do?"

Again Kate nodded.

"I happened to be in the same pub as Craig one night. He'd just been given the heave ho! And cursing all and sundry. I heard Josephine Grace's name, so I went and had a chat. A few pints later and I had the whole story." He shook his head and looked down at his hands that had become clenched. Consciously relaxing them, he continued, "I just knew Craig would not be her only victim. I watched the way people became flavour of the month and then backed off. Some of the jibes in my missives were guess work but I don't think I was too wide of the mark, was I?"

"What about the early stuff, when Sally Price was at school?" Colm interjected.

Miller smirked, not a pleasant expression on his normally kind face. "I talked to people. There was a writer who had written her official biography. You'd be surprised what people make you leave out when they're paying the bill."

"But they told you?"

"A little liquid and financial persuasion opened Pandora's box! I even found a couple of old school mates. They'd never linked Sally Price to Josey Grace but were happy to gossip!"

Kate refrained from commenting and Miller filled the gap. "She was a wicked woman. I did give her a chance to mend her ways but she refused my suggestions."

"So you killed her?" Kate threw the grenade in.

Silence.

Miller looked her square in the eye. "Am I under arrest?"

"Not yet but I would like to continue this conversation back at the station."

"In that case I'll wait until I have spoken with a legal representative before we go on."

CHAPTER 65

Miller sat calmly in the interview room while he waited for his lawyer. He had declined the offer of the police on call solicitor and that of a drink. He seemed very relaxed as Kate and Colm observed him through the two-way mirror. "He doesn't look particularly worried," said Colm, "Do you think he did it?"

"I'm sure he did. It's whether he confesses or we have to break down every lie as we go."

"He was up front about the letters."

"Umm. But as we've said before, there's nothing in any of them that can be construed as a definite threat of harm. I'm going to have a quick chat with Mike in forensics."

Kate left and quickly hurried upstairs to Mike's office, praying that he would be available. He was.

"Hi Kate? How's it going? The rumour mill says you have a suspect in."

Kate smiled. Mike's team may appear cut off from the rest of the station but if you wanted the latest on any subject, they would know!

"Quick questions before I go back and try and get a confession: how long could forensics survive in the back of a work's van?"

"Like three years?"

Kate nodded.

Mike ran his hands over his hair, combing a few wayward strands over his growing bald patch. "We might get very lucky and find a hair caught on a rough patch but anything else, I'm doubtful."

Kate screwed up her nose. "Pretty much what I feared."

"But we'd give it a go if you needed it," Mike said helpfully.

"Thanks Mike, leave it for now but would you get a snapper out to the victim's house and photograph the back lane. I want to show that her garden is the only one that's regularly been using it."

"No problem. I've got a fast tracker in; she can give it a go."

Kate waved a hand in farewell and appreciation. If she couldn't get Miller to open up she might have to have a long shot and see if the van held anything. Remote as that chance might be.

Kate met Colm climbing the stairs. "Miller's solicitor is in and talking with him. I thought I'd grab a coffee. Do you want one?"

"Yes. I'll take another look at the murder board. Check for anything we might have missed."

Kate turned on the step and led Colm up to the incident room. She walked across to the board while Colm coaxed two coffees from the machine. Carrying them carefully he joined Kate at the board and handed her one of the cups. "There you go."

"Thanks Colm." Kate continued to stare at the board. "We have a motive and we have means. We know a van, that Miller had access to, was parked in the lane around nine-thirty on the evening our victim was murdered. What we don't know is whether it was still there at two. We know Miller, as Rogers, worked for a biotech company that was researching the mycelium. Did Miller work on that project or know about it?"

Kate broke off and called across, "Alice would you ring Mark Masefield, the HR manager at Biotech Solutions and ask him which projects Rogers worked on. See if there is a link to the mycelium research. Sorry, I should have done that earlier."

"No problem, boss," called Alice, already reaching for her desk phone.

"Miller may have learnt about the field and the tree preservation order when out with his Rambler buddies and he'd been in the area for five years when Grace disappeared."

Colm looked over the board and nodded, "We just don't have any physical evidence that ties Miller to the body or its transportation. What did Mike say?"

Kate shrugged, "He'd give it a try if it was a last resort." As she said these words a thought fired in her head. She called across, "Len, will you give Hugh Gifford a ring? See if you can get any more details about the man he saw smoking in Grace's garden on the evening of the party."

Len nodded and held up a hand in acknowledgement whilst the other one clicked his mouse.

The telephone on Kate's desk rang and she swiftly answered it. Putting it back down, she said, "Miller and his solicitor are ready." Kate looked across at Alice but she was still in conversation on the phone. Kate knew Alice would bring the information to her when she had it.

"Come on then. Time for battle."

CHAPTER 66

For the benefit of the tap, Kate introduced everyone in the room. Before she could speak further, Miller's solicitor cleared his throat, "My client would like to make a statement." He then proceeded to read from the paper in front of him. "My client admits to writing the letters to Josephine Grace but he denies that they were threatening or that he was responsible for the subsequent death of Ms Grace."

Short and sweet, Kate thought. Pretty much what she expected from Miller. She would have advised the same thing if she had been giving him legal support. Now, she had to break him down and find the real Will Miller and the passion that drove him to kill. And it was premeditated. The mycelium matting was proof of that. Grace's death had not been a spur of the moment event. Miller had planned.

"Thank you for that, Mr Miller. Would you explain why you wrote the letters, please?"

Kate could see the suspicion in Miller's eyes. He began slowly, thinking about each word. "I thought Josephine Grace needed reminding of how she'd got to her position and how many people she had hurt on her way up the ladder."

"That's why you signed off using the nom de plume of Your Conscience?"

Miller nodded but Kate continued, "But how was Ms Grace to show you that she was thinking about what she had done or that she might want to make reparation. She had no way of contacting you."

Miller snorted. "I watched her; she wasn't thinking about reparation."

"Weren't the letters more about giving Ms Grace a taste of her own medicine? To know that someone had information on her that would lead to her humiliation?"

Miller smiled, "I suppose there was an element of that, yes."

"So you didn't really want her to mend her ways at all!" Kate stated. "So what was the *purpose* of the letters?" Kate emphasised.

Miller shrugged. "If I'm honest, I just wanted to let her know what had happened to Sylvie and that someone knew what she was really like."

"That would be Sylvie Hardcastle, your birth mother?"

Miller sighed and nodded.

"For the benefit of the tape, please, Mr Miller," Kate said pointing at the tape.

Another sigh and, "Yes!"

Kate tried another tack, "The last letter did have tones of *or else* didn't it?"

Another shrug.

"What had you planned if she didn't retire? You must have had a Plan B. You've carefully set everything up, I can't imagine that you hadn't planned for her refusal. In fact I think you knew she'd refuse to retire. She'd call your bluff. So why didn't you reveal all?"

"She disappeared, didn't she?"

"Surely that would have made your news even more explosive, wouldn't it? Her name in all the papers and your revelation, perfect."

Yet another shrug. "I didn't kill her."

"So what was Plan B?"

"I didn't have one."

It was Kate's turn to snort, "Oh come on, Mr Miller. You're a planner. You're a doer. You couldn't let it go out like a damp squib. So what did you do? Wait until after the party and go and talk with her?"

"You have a very vivid imagination Detective Inspector Medlar."

A complete change of direction, Kate decided. "I understand you had access to the Duckets' works van the week of Ms Grace's disappearance. Is that correct?"

Kate thought she saw Miller's eyes open slightly wider and he adjusted his position in his chair. His solicitor, who had kept his head down and focused on his notes, now looked up and gave his client a glance.

Miller hedged his bets, "Was it that week I drove their van? I'd forgotten."

Kate made a play of looking through her notes. "Ah, yes. Joey Duckets broke his leg on the Tuesday of that week and you drove their van for eleven days."

Another shrug. "Okay, I'll take your word for it."

"Yes and you see there was a complaint made about the van blocking the back lane to Ms Grace's home."

Miller frowned. "I only parked it there a couple of times."

Three times, in fact," Kate looked at her papers again. "The afternoons of Tuesday and Wednesday of that week." Kate watched as Miller relaxed and then she went in for the kill, "and the evening of Friday, August 15, when Ms Grace disappeared and was murdered."

Kate watched as Miller's hands clutched into fists and he fought the jerk in his left leg. She continued probing, "Can you explain about the Friday evening, Mr Miller?"

Miller looked directly at her and then leant to whisper into his solicitor's ear. In turn he spoke to Kate, "My client would like a comfort break, please, Inspector."

CHAPTER 67

Kate and Colm reconvened in the observation room. As he shut the door, Colm said, "He wasn't expecting that and he doesn't know what time he was observed."

"Um," Kate looked thoughtful. "He'll be using this time to come up with an explanation, I'm sure."

"Of course he is. Ay up! They're back in."

Kate repeated the tape introductions and gave the time before recapping on her last question, "So can you explain why the van you had access to was behind Ms Grace's home on Friday evening?"

Miller's body language was confident now, he thought he had her, "I parked it there for safety."

"Safety? Could you explain that, please?" Kate hoped that her disbelief was evident.

"The van had been broken into at the Duckets yard and I was worried it would happen again."

"So parking in an infrequently used back lane is safer than parking in the drive of your own home? I really find that hard to comprehend."

A nonchalant shrug. He knew he didn't need to prove it, she had to disprove it.

"In the time you had access to this van, did Ms Grace ever have cause to be in the van?"

Miller looked wary. "No."

"You're sure about that? You're a scientist, Mr Miller. You know how forensics work. Don't you?"

He was uncomfortable again. He didn't know she had nothing but she could just sow a seed of doubt. Her game plan was interrupted by a brisk knock on the door. Kate called them in and Alice entered. "For the benefit of the tape, Police Constable Giles has entered."

Kate took the two slips of paper Alice offered and read quickly. Alice received a half smile as Kate closed the door, passing the papers to Colm, who raised his eyebrows as he read.

"What time did you park the van in that back lane, Mr Miller? That Friday evening?"

Miller rubbed his nose with one hand. "I'm not a hundred per cent sure but I think about nine-thirtyish."

"Did you pop into the garden at all while you were there?"

Again a hesitation. Kate knew he was weighing up how much he needed to tell. Finally, "Yes, I believe I did. Just interested to see what the party was like."

"Did you go up to the house?"

Again, there was a delay in the reply. "I went as far as the azalea bushes at the edge of the lawn."

"Did you see anyone? Or anyone see you?"

"No. I wasn't supposed to be there so I hung about in the shadows."

"In fact you were seen that evening, in the garden. A witness has given quite a detailed statement." Kate waved one of Alice's pieces of paper.

Miller shrugged. Kate knew that all Gifford had done was confirm Miller's timings and actions. She continued, "So how long were you there for? Did you hear Ms Grace's speech?"

A weary, or was it a wary, nod of the head.

"For the tape please, Mr Miller."

"Yes, I heard it."

"Didn't that make you angry? No mention of retirement?"

A forced sigh, "I hadn't really expected her to make the announcement."

"So that brings me back to my previous question. What was Plan B?"

A hint of anger, "I didn't have a Plan B."

"All that planning. All that anger at what she had done to your birth mother and to the other people you found out about and you were just going to let it go?" Kate heightened her incredulity.

"I did not have a Plan B. I did not kill her."

Miller's solicitor intervened. "My client has answered the same question several times, Inspector. Unless you have evidence to disprove my client's claim, may I suggest we move on."

Kate was frustrated. She knew if she kept on at Miller his anger would get the better of him. She could feel it simmering, just under control.

Okay, if the solicitor wasn't going to allow that line of enquiry, she'd call a break now.

CHAPTER 68

Kate headed for the car park. She needed to walk and stretch the frustration from her body. Colm followed and patiently leaned against a wall while Kate strode back and forth rotating her neck and shoulders. Finally, Kate stopped in front of him. "I've got the psychology wrong."

Colm raised an eyebrow and waited.

Kate continued, "Why didn't he release all the information when Grace went missing?"

"Because he knew Grace was already dead."

"But if his aim was to besmirch her name, wouldn't he have still wanted the public to know? Whether she was missing or dead?"

Colm carefully considered before replying. "You don't think it was about *pay back* with our victim?"

Kate strode away and back again before she answered, "No. I am sure he wanted her to suffer the anxiety of someone having something over her but what do the letters want her to do?"

"Stop and retire."

Kate halted her pacing again. "Exactly! To stop."

"So when she didn't announce her retirement at the party she had to be stopped?"

"But why did she have to be stopped?"

Colm's face and tone conveyed his

incredulity, "Because it's illegal. It's immoral."

"Yes, yes. That's all very laudable but does Miller seem that type?"

Colm looked nonplussed, "I'm not sure I understand what you're on about, boss."

It was Kate's turn to look thoughtful. An idea was appearing on the horizon of her mind. Miller hadn't killed for these high ideals. There was something much more personal about strangling someone. Who did he want to protect? It wasn't his birth mother, she was already dead. So who? And then it came to her.

"Colm, when we go back in I'm going to introduce the mycelium shroud idea but I'm sure Miller will close that down. Then I'm going to ask the questions I've just asked of you. Then you and I are going to leave the interview. When I go back in you're going to say something like, 'Summer Loving, you want her in?' Loud enough for Miller to hear as well. Okay?"

"You think he's protecting Summer Loving? Does he even know her?"

"We're going to find out. Come on."

Kate skipped up the stairs to her office. "Alice, will you contact Claire Bayntry and find out whether Miller and Summer Loving knew one another - you know, were they friends?"

Alice's face showed that she was as sceptical as Colm had been at the suggestion. "Yes, boss. Do you want me to interrupt your interview when I have the information?"

"Yes, please. As soon as you can. Right. Let's see if we can find Miller's weak spot." Kate was on her way out the door when she stopped so suddenly that Colm, following, almost knocked her over. She turned back to Alice, "No, don't interrupt the interview. Just knock on the door and wait." Kate turned to Colm, "That will be the point at which we have our little play."

CHAPTER 69

Back in the interview room Kate rearranged her papers and began. "Mr Miller, I understand that as Mr Tom Rogers you worked for Biotech Solutions. Is that correct?"

"Yes, but I don't see."

Kate cut across him. "It is relevant Mr Miller. Would you explain the projects you were involved in whilst you were there?"

"Not really. We have to sign a clause to guard against industrial espionage."

It was Kate's turn to sign, "Mr Miller. We are not interested in the minutiae of your work. Just some broad strokes to give us an idea of the work you did."

Miller held his hands up, palms facing Kate. "Okay." His tone indicated that he was humouring her. "I worked in the biochemical side of the industry and was involved in a number of projects. Many involved eco effective activities."

Colm interrupted, "Eco effective?"

Miller sighed and his tone became condescending to the point of insult. "Yes. The whole world wants things to be eco-friendly or to have limited impact on the environment; how to clean up oil after a spillage at sea, how to prevent micro-plastics forming, that sort of thing."

Kate looked at Alice's slip of paper, "And mycelium shrouds?"

Again Kate had placed an unexpected blow. Miller rallied. "Yes. That was one of the projects I worked on."

"Oh. Mr Miller, you are being too modest. The shroud was your baby. You took the lead, I understand."

This time it was Miller's solicitor's turn to interrupt, "Inspector I fail to see how my client's past skills are related to your ongoing murder investigation."

Kate smiled pleasantly. "Well you see, in layman's terms, the body of Ms Grace was found with the remains of a mycelium shroud. Now as I am sure your client can explain to you, these items are not widely known about by the public. They are still in the very early stages of development," Kate turned to Miller, "aren't they Mr Miller?"

Miller had paled. Kate watched. Had he thought they would not investigate everything? Had he really thought they would not make the Rogers/Miller connection?

There was a deafening silence. Kate was happy to let Miller wallow. Eventually, he managed, "Yes, I was very involved in the mycelium shroud project but you would need to have access to just the right environment to successfully create one."

Kate perused Alice's note again. "Really?

According to Biotech, a damp cellar with sufficient darkness and a supply of mushrooms and feed and you're away. It's one of the reasons Biotech are so keen to develop this further. Isn't that so?"

Kate noted a bead of sweat appear on Miller's top lip and she pushed her point. "Weren't you telling us about your damp cellar?"

Colm kept up the pressure, "A cellar. Dark and damp. Perfect mushroom growing conditions."

Miller tried to blind them with science, "The growing of the mycelium is the easy part. The difficult part is drying it out."

Kate continued pushing, "2015 was quite a good summer, if I remember rightly. Hot days, wouldn't that dry out your shroud."

There was a soft knock at the door, which Kate ignored.

Miller's solicitor broke in to the conversation, "Inspector, my client has not admitted to growing such an item. Neither have you established a motive for him in wanting Josephine Grace dead."

Kate could have kissed him. A perfect opening. "You are correct," Kate turned back to Miller, "and I have been puzzling over your motivation. Why would you want Grace dead? Revenge?" Kate shook her head. "You wanted her to stop. To retire. To stop having influence."

"All that happened when she disappeared," Miller said.

Kate nodded, "But a disappearance would only be a temporary reprieve, wouldn't it? She would have to be dead in order for people to be safe from her grip." Kate hoped she sounded like she was musing out loud. She'd never been very good at acting but now she hoped her face was showing dawning light. "Protect someone?" She looked hard at Miller, who deliberately avoided eye contact. Kate made a decisive move to rise and announced, "Interview suspended for ten minutes. Detectives Medlar and Hunter exiting the interview room."

Kate and Colm stepped out and the duty constable stepped into the room. Alice was waiting impatiently. "I don't know how you knew, boss but Miller and Loving were quite pally in the summer of 2015." Alice checked her notes, "Apparently Loving went to stay with Grace during the summer of that year and she would often go out into the garden and talk with Miller. Quite a friendship developed."

"Romantic?" Colm asked.

"I asked that, but no. Ms Bayntry said, it was more like a father daughter thing."

"So you think Miller killed Grace to protect Summer Loving?" Colm addressed Kate.

Kate nodded. "Yes I do. Now we need him to think she's under suspicion. Ready?"

CHAPTER 70

Kate re-entered the interview room. As she closed the door everyone could clearly hear Colm say, "Summer Loving? Okay boss."

Kate closed the door quickly as though wanting to drown out Colm's voice but knowing that Miller had definitely heard. He had immediately tensed and Kate saw him drop his clenched fists into his lap. She hoped she was right about this.

"Now Mr Miller. The mycelium shroud."

"Why are you involving Summer?"

Kate played at surprise, "Ms Loving? I wasn't aware that you knew her."

Miller tried to play his interest down. "She stopped with Ms Grace that summer and I had a few chats with her."

"Oh right. Now this shroud."

Miller interrupted again, "What about Summer?"

Kate leant back in her chair and played her hand, "It occurred to me, as I was talking with you, that of all the people we have talked to in this case the one who has the most to lose is Ms Loving."

"But you think I grew the shroud."

"Yes. Perhaps you were in it together, or perhaps Ms Loving found out about the shroud and stole it from you. You could clarify those points for me."

The solicitor interrupted again, "So are you now not considering my client as the murderer of Ms Grace?"

Kate stared him down, "We are now considering that this might be a case of joint enterprise."

Miller turned to his solicitor, "What does that mean? Joint enterprise?"

Kate answered for him, "That you assisted Ms Loving in the murder and disposal of Ms Grace's body."

"Summer had nothing to do with it." The words were flat and unemotional.

Kate acted surprised again. "How do you know this Mr Miller?"

Miller leant back in his chair and closed his eyes. He took in several deep breaths and the tension left his body. He sat up straight and opening his eyes, clearly said, "I murdered Josephine Grace in the early hours of Saturday, August 16, 2015." His solicitor tried to stop him continuing but Miller continued, "I wrapped her in a mycelium shroud in the van I was using from Duckets. I drove her out to Knight's Halt and buried her by a crop of trees." As though exhausted he sat back again and closed his eyes.

Kate was exultant. She was sure Colm, and probably Alice were in the observation room, cheering. "Thank you for your honesty, Mr

Miller. Would you explain why you murdered Josephine Grace?"

Miller was listless, "What does it matter? She's dead and I killed her."

"But why?" Kate persisted.

"She was a vile woman who fed on the misery of others. She made my birth mother suffer untold anguish and betrayed people who trusted her with their friendship. She deserved to die."

Kate beckoned at the two way mirror. Seconds later Colm appeared in the room. "Colm, would you formerly arrest Mr Miller and place him in a cell, please."

Colm took hold of Miller's arm as he rose from his chair and read him his rights before leading him out. Kate watched as Miller's solicitor packed away his notebooks and pens. When he was ready he stood and offered Kate his hand. "Well done, Inspector Medlar. Mr Miller will now need a specialist legal team so I won't be seeing you again," he smiled and walked out.

Kate slowly stood and stretched. It was the psychology she had got wrong to start with. Now she needed to present their case to the CPS. With the confession she was sure they would charge and prosecute.

2am Saturday, August 16, 2015

Summer Loving stole quietly down the stairs.

Fighting with Josey and losing her temper was not going to work. She needed to be calm and play to Josey's professionalism. She hadn't heard Josey come up and the lights were still on, so Summer sought her out.

Josey was still sat in her chair, in the lounge, enjoying a glass of brandy. She looked up and smiled as Summer came through the door.

"Would you like a night cap?" *she asked as if their heated words of half an hour ago had never been.*

"No, thanks, Josey. Could we talk about your proposal again, please?"

"Of course my dear. I want a role in your latest play. The mother-in-law would be perfect. I am the right age and my name is still recognised by theatregoers."

Inwardly Summer sighed, "I know that's what you would like but I don't have the power to influence the director. This is my first leading role."

"Now, my dear. Don't be so gutless. All you have to do is drop my name into the conversation. Suggest how wonderful I would be. Perhaps even sell a sob story about paying back someone who has been so influential in your career." *This last part was said with a certain edge.*

Summer shook her head. She was not going to change Josey's mind. "I'm sorry, Josey, I can't. And if that means you tell the world about my abortion, then so be it." *With that Summer got up and left.*

Josey's words followed her, "You will be sorry!"

In the hall, Josey found Will Miller. He looked as if he had been there for a little while. He must have heard everything. She frowned in surprise. "Will, what are you doing here?"

Will put his finger to his lips and quietly said, "I have something to discuss with Ms Grace." He turned purposefully for the lounge door and said, "Goodnight Summer, off to bed now."

Summer climbed the stairs slowly. She heard the surprise in Josey's voice as Will went in. On the landing Summer stopped and leant over the banister trying to listen to their conversation but all she could hear was the rise and fall of their voices. Reluctantly, she turned to her bedroom. She'd talk to Will over the weekend and check out what he had heard.

CHAPTER 71

The memorial for Josephine Grace was not the lavish affair she would have wanted it to be. Many former fans had read about her deeds when news of the arrest of Will Miller for her murder was released. Kate was sure it was a public relations scam by Miller's legal team. Interestingly, many of Grace's former victims did attend; Salisbury, Purcell, Loving and Gifford.

"Just to check she's really dead," Colm had wickedly suggested.

Kate caught sight of Loving on her own. Excusing herself from Colm's company she headed towards her. "Ms Loving!"

Loving turned and smiled, "Detective Inspector Medlar. So it's true, police do attend the victim's funeral."

"Yes, mostly. Have you got five minutes?"

Loving frowned but nodded as Kate led them to a path away from the main one. They strolled along it and Kate began, "You knew Will Miller was our murderer, didn't you?"

Loving did not answer immediately. "I thought it probable," she finally offered.

"And yet you chose not to tell us?"

Loving stopped. "I know I should have done but Will was a friend and Josey was a wicked woman. And, I suppose, I thought I owed him. He never mentioned what he must have overheard and he could have done."

Kate shook her head. "You could be charged with being an accessory."

Loving looked scared and Kate waved her hand. "I can't prove that you knew and it would serve no justice I understand to involve you as well."

"Thank you, DI Medlar." Loving held out a hand, which Kate took and shook before leaving Loving on the path. It had been a guess about Loving being there but it made more sense given Miller's actions and reactions.

She reached Colm who was waiting by their car. "Come on, then Colm. We've done our bit."

MEDLAR 3

DI Kate Medlar will return in A Long Game...

ALSO FROM TIM SAUNDERS
PUBLICATIONS

Love and Death by Iain Curr
The Fourth Rising Trilogy by Tom Beardsell
Letters from Chapel Farm by Mary Buchan
That was now, this is then
by Philip Dawson-Hammond
Heathcare Heroes by Dr Mark Rickenbach
Shadows and Daisies by Sharon Webster
Lomax at War by Dan Boylan
A Life Worth Living by Mary Cochrane
Faze by MJ White
A Dream of Destiny by DoLoraVi
Dreams Can Come True by Rebecca Mansell
The Collected Works of TA Saunders

tsaunderspubs.weebly.com

Unsolicited manuscripts welcome

THE PAUL CAVE PRIZE FOR LITERATURE

The Paul Cave Prize for Literature, established in 2023 by Tim Saunders Publications, is in memory of Paul Astley Cave-Browne-Cave (1917 to 2010), a hugely inspirational magazine and book publisher. In 1960 Paul founded Hampshire the county magazine, running it for over 40 years. Paul was keen to help those who had the drive and determination to succeed, which is what this prize is all about.

What we are looking for:
All forms of poetry: haiku, free verse, sonnet, acrostic, villanelle, ballad, limerick, ode, elegy, flash fiction, short stories and novellas in any genre except erotic. Work must be new and unpublished. International submissions welcome.

Guidelines
Poems
should not exceed 30 lines

Flash fiction
should not exceed 300 words

Short stories
should not exceed 1,000 words

Novellas
should not exceed 10,000 words

Prizes
Best Novella - £100
Best Short Story - £50
Best Flash Fiction - £25
Best Poem - £25

Winners of each category will have their work published on this web page and will receive a complimentary copy of The Paul Cave Prize for Literature 2023 book to be published by the end of 2023.

All approved submissions will feature in The Paul Cave Prize for Literature 2023. Each writer who submits a piece of approved work is guaranteed to have it published in the book.

How to enter
1. email your submission(s) to tsaunderspubs@gmail.com
2. send payment by Paypal to tsaunderspubs@gmail.com

For more information visit:
tsaunderspubs.weebly.com

Printed in Great Britain
by Amazon